HER HIGHLAND LAIRD

Fleeing her unfaithful fiancé, Lara sticks a pin in the map and vows to go wherever it lands. She finds herself in the cool summer of the Scottish Highlands, landing a job at Invermalloch Estate. Here, she meets Cal, the brooding Laird who is hiding from his own painful past. A powerful attraction between them slowly turns to love. But when Cal is called back to America, will this love survive — or will Lara's Highland Laird prove to be only a summer romance?

CAROL MacLEAN

HER HIGHLAND LAIRD

Complete and Unabridged

LINFORD
Leicester

First published in Great Britain in 2016

First Linford Edition
published 2016

A catalogue record for this book is available
from the British Library.

ISBN 978–1–4448–2947–1

Published by
F. A. Thorpe (Publishing)
Anstey, Leicestershire

Set by Words & Graphics Ltd.
Anstey, Leicestershire
Printed and bound in Great Britain by
T. J. International Ltd., Padstow, Cornwall

This book is printed on acid-free paper

1

Lara stepped onto the platform and the train's doors swished shut behind her. Within minutes the train was gone, leaving behind it nothing but a taint of diesel and a mournful hoot lingering on the air. She looked around and shivered. There was no-one around in the country station. The ticket office was cute, like a gingerbread house, and there were three well-tended pots of colourful summer flowers outside it. But there was a cold breeze and the sun was hidden behind dull grey clouds. So much for summer in Scotland. *And that's what I get for sticking a pin in the map to choose my escape,* she thought wryly. Briefly, she imagined the hot sunshine she'd left behind in Devon. But that wouldn't do. Other recent memories flooded into her mind too and she pushed them down hard. She wasn't here to think about that. She was here to make a fresh start.

Slinging her rucksack onto her back, she walked out of the station and onto the pavement of a settlement too small even to be a village. It was simply a scattering of houses which fringed a ribbon of road. Beyond the last house the road wound its way through rough moorland and up over a rise. Glad of her stout walking boots, she took a deep breath and followed it towards a backdrop of distant mountains.

She fumbled in her pocket for the piece of paper she'd been given. A woman she'd met on the train had told her there were jobs at the Invermalloch Estate. She'd kindly scribbled a loose description of how to get there for Lara and wished her luck. Lara was beginning to think she'd need it. Only one car had passed her. It was a lonely, harsh and bleak place. She gripped the straps of her rucksack more tightly, feeling the strain of its weight on her back. She hadn't brought much, just shoved essentials into it and hardly seeing what she was doing through the blur of tears. Wherever she ended up, she could send for her stuff then. As usual she'd acted on blind impulse. She had to get away. End of story.

But where had she landed up? She'd taken her map of Britain and a glass-headed dressmaker's pin and sworn to herself that wherever it landed, she'd go and no excuses. Squeezing her eyes shut, she'd stuck it into the paper with savagery. The Highlands. It sounded far away and she'd never been there. Perfect. Except the reality was different. It was hardly like the Britain she knew. There was a coldness to the landscape as if nature was indifferent to her fate. She shivered again at the sight of the dark, jagged outlines of the mountains. They looked dramatic and dangerous.

A blue car drew up beside her and the driver's window was wound down.

'Hello, can I offer you a lift somewhere?'

The woman was a little older than Lara, maybe early thirties, with short, blonde curly hair and laughing brown eyes. Gratefully, Lara opened the passenger door and slid in, tucking her rucksack at her feet.

'I'm trying to get to Invermalloch Estate. Is that on your way?'

The woman looked at her with more interest and held out her hand.

'I'm Helen Thorpe. You're very lucky because I'm headed exactly for Invermalloch, which is where I work. Can I ask why you're going?'

'I'm Lara Haynes,' Lara said, shaking Helen's hand in greeting. 'I'm hoping there may be a job there for me. Do you know the owner?'

Helen Thorpe pushed her foot down and the car sped along the road. She glanced at Lara briefly. 'Invermalloch's owned by the local Laird. That's the Scottish for 'Lord',' she smiled, clearly having picked up on Lara's English accent.

Lara smiled back. Helen was so

friendly and warm, she liked her immediately. She pictured the Laird as an old, crusty gentleman, with white whiskers and a mustard-coloured tweed jacket.

'So, should I ask for him when I get to the estate?' she enquired hopefully.

Helen shook her head and frowned darkly. 'Oh no, he doesn't deal with staffing. He's not . . . not well, poor soul.'

Lara added a heart condition to her tweedy, whiskered old gentleman, and felt quite sorry for him.

'It'll be myself that deals with you,' Helen said, a melodic Highland lilt to her voice. 'I'm secretary to the estate manager, and I do the hiring and firing. Not that we fire much; we're a reasonably happy bunch, and it's a nice place to work.' She laughed.

Lara felt reassured by that. Just as she was about to ask Helen if there was a seasonal ranger's post available, the car swung left through an enormous set of stone gateposts. She had time to see there were heraldry shields on top of the posts, and a long fence of wrought iron, before they were zooming along an endless driveway which ended in front of a huge gothic mansion.

'Invermalloch Lodge,' Helen said proudly.

It was a building of carved stone towers, lots of windows, and occasional gargoyles glaring from the ancient drainage pipes. A confectionary of a house, as if each generation of owners had added their own fanciful wing or extension. Lara grabbed her rucksack and forced herself not to feel daunted by such obvious age and status and wealth.

She turned to find Helen watching her. Lara gave a small smile. It felt wobbly. *I will not cry. I will not think of Jason and Kate. Of Malorie and Mum and Dad. I need to do this.* She pressed her lips together and lifted her head confidently, even though her stomach roiled like a dozen bunched snakes.

'Sorry Lara, I've a few duties to take

care of before I can chat with you about our seasonal vacancies. Would you mind waiting ten minutes for me? If you like, you can take a look round the stables while you wait. Just round there.' Helen pointed apologetically in the direction of another set of buildings.

'That's fine,' Lara said, hiding her relief. She'd take the ten minutes gratefully and attempt to calm down. She wanted to come across as capable and responsible when Helen interviewed her. She needed a job. There was no going back to Devon. And, despite Malorie's views on it, she was never going to forgive Jason for what he'd done.

The stables were set around a cobbled courtyard. There was a smell of hay and horse and old leather. A few horses snickered and pushed their heads towards her from their stalls as she ventured in. She was drawn to the far stall. There was a beautiful sable horse with a gleaming coat. Lara loved animals, big and small. She had never had much to do with horses, but that didn't matter. She went across to the black animal and raised her hand to stroke his nose.

'Don't touch him!' a man's voice barked at her.

Startled, Lara turned to see a tall figure striding towards them. She had a moment to notice a slight limp before he was right there, towering over her. An unwelcome flicker of attraction rippled through her. He was tall, at least six foot two, with broad shoulders. His hair was thick and curled and as dark as the horse's pelt. But where the horse had gentle brown eyes, this man's were piercing blue and none too friendly. His jaw was tight and there was a dark shadow of stubble as if he hadn't shaved that day.

'I wasn't going to harm him,' Lara said, standing her ground despite the man being right inside her personal space. She could almost feel the air between them bristle.

'A little thing like you couldn't harm

Kinash.' There was a tint of something, amusement perhaps, in his tone. Or was it derision? She couldn't help noticing how deep his voice was, and the velvet of an accent she couldn't quite place. Transatlantic of some sort, but with a Scottish edge to it.

'What's the problem, then?' Lara asked, tilting her face to stare directly at him. Who was he anyway? The estate manager that Helen Thorpe had referred to? Or an overzealous stable boy? Lara smiled inwardly. There was no 'boy' about this man. He had an air of authority about him.

'Just . . . don't touch him. Please.'

The 'please' had cost him, Lara thought, annoyed. She should have moved away and left it at that. But, *really*. She hadn't been doing anything wrong. She was filling her ten-minute wait, bothering no one and minding her own business. He was the one who'd come barging in, bossing her about!

'You need to tell me why. Why can't I touch him?' Lara could almost see

Malorie shaking her head and telling her she was too stubborn for her own good.

He sighed and ran his fingers through his hair, making it look rakish and him even more darkly attractive. Now Lara was annoyed at herself as much as at him. She'd no intention of finding men desirable ever again. She was sworn off them. Her anger made her stand there, hands on hips, waiting for his answer. There was no way she'd let him see the effect he had on her.

'It's for your own good,' he said, sounding weary. 'Kinash is very highly strung. You risk a nip at best if you go near him. At worst, he could injure you and himself if he gets upset.'

'Oh.' Lara could think of nothing else to add to that.

Bother. She wanted to think the worst of him. He was a man, after all, and Jason had put her off the whole species. But instead, she felt a sudden pity. There were deeply grooved lines around his mouth as if he suffered pain.

She again saw the limp as he turned from her, and wondered what had caused it.

'Do you work here?' she called after him.

He hesitated, then turned back. She felt the full blast of those sharp blue eyes upon her. She thought of clear winter skies and cold Scottish lochs, then felt the heat rise in her face at his scrutiny. Did the man never smile?

'There you are, I'm ready for you now.' Helen Thorpe appeared in the courtyard with a smile for Lara, then glanced between the two of them. 'You've met the Laird, then. That's good.' She nodded to him. 'Cal, there are a few calls for you. I said you'd phone back.'

He was the Laird? But he couldn't be more than thirty! The image of the sweet old gentleman crumbled away to be replaced with the darkly brooding man in front of her. Lara shut her mouth, aware she'd opened it in astonishment.

'Thank you, Helen. Please tell the callers I'm unavailable. I'm sure you and Bob can handle whatever it is between you.' His tone for Helen Thorpe was quite different to the way he'd spoken to Lara. It was even and calm and pleasant.

Helen sighed as they watched the tall figure walk away, his shoulders stiffly held ramrod-straight as if in compensation for the limp.

'He doesn't make it easy on himself,' Helen said, shaking her head sadly. With visible effort, she put on a polite smile for Lara. 'Now, would you like to come inside, and we'll have a wee chat about our vacancies?'

Lara would have liked to ask what Helen meant about the Laird. He didn't make it easy on himself — what was that all about? But she followed the older woman back to the main house. It wasn't her place to ask, and it was none of her concern. She was here to get a job, that was all that mattered. She dampened down her curiosity. She was hardly likely to see him much anyway, if he was the Laird and she was just a hired seasonal.

The inside of Invermalloch Lodge was just as eccentric as the exterior. The hallway was lined with an ancient, faded red carpet which smelt of old dust and mould. A series of suits of armour stood against the long walls like sentries. The hallway widened out into a huge room with black-and-white flagged tiles and a monstrous fireplace. Above the fireplace were a variety of stuffed animal heads mounted on wooden plates. Lara grimaced. How awful. These were clearly hunting trophies.

Helen noticed her expression. 'Horrid, aren't they? But I'm afraid that Invermalloch is originally a Victorian hunting lodge. The Lairds back then lived in the south, and only came up here with their friends to hunt and shoot and fish for entertainment.'

'Do the Laird and his family live here now?' Lara asked, horribly fascinated by the decor.

'The family live in America. There's only Cal here, for a short while.' Helen pursed her lips as if she'd already said too much. 'Come along, we'll go in here to my office.'

Helen's office was in a side room on the left. In contrast to the large room, it was small and cosy and cheerful, with modern furniture, a vase of flowers, and framed prints on the walls. Helen settled herself into the chair at the desk and gestured to Lara to take the other.

'Now, what kind of job are you looking for? We're not taking on as many workers this year, I'm afraid.'

'I was hoping you might be able to use a wildlife ranger,' Lara said. In her experience, many large estates and country parks employed a ranger to look after the animals and plants, and take educational tours for the public and interested groups.

'A wildlife ranger?' Helen sounded doubtful. 'I'm not sure we've had one before.'

'If Invermalloch is as large it appears,

then a ranger is a real asset,' Lara said enthusiastically. 'I can assess the habitats and help bring in revenue, such as funding for conservation works, by taking tours which people pay to attend.'

'What's your previous work experience?' Helen asked, neatly swerving any ready answer.

Lara undid the clasp on her rucksack and found her papers. Luckily she had two excellent references from her ranger job in Sussex. She'd loved that job, and had only given it up at Jason's persuading. How she regretted that now. Back then, it had made sense. She gave them over to Helen, who took her time reading them carefully.

She looked up eventually and smiled. 'Well, you do seem to have a lot of good skills, and according to this you're a dedicated and efficient worker. But I don't know whether Invermalloch needs a ranger.'

Lara's heart sank. She'd hoped to find a place here. Where would she go if

Helen didn't take her on? It was getting late in the day to go elsewhere but if she had to, then she'd head further north. The stubbornness Malorie complained of stood Lara in good stead at times like these. She wouldn't give up. She wouldn't return south to her old life. She was adamant about that.

'Let me have a think about it,' Helen went on kindly. 'I'll speak to Cal about you and he can make the decision.'

Lara doubted Cal would want to take her on. He came across as a bad-tempered, arrogant man — even if he was dangerously good-looking and attractive. He didn't want her near his horse, and he didn't look like the type to care about nature.

'It's getting late.' Helen stood up, indicating that the short interview was over. 'Have you got a place to stay tonight?'

'I'll be fine,' Lara lied, hoisting her rucksack back onto her shoulder.

Helen Thorpe didn't owe her anything. Lara had tried and lost at

Invermalloch. She just might have better luck elsewhere. She planned to go back to the tiny village and find a hostel, or a bed-and-breakfast place. Tomorrow, she'd take the train north. From her hazy recollection of the timetable she was already as far north and west as possible by train track.

'Can you drop by tomorrow for an answer?' Helen asked, showing her out.

'Yes. Thank you.' Lara didn't trust herself to say more. There was a threadiness to her voice which appalled her. There was no way she wanted to cry in front of this kind woman.

* * *

Cal MacDonald swore fiercely under his breath and kicked the chair with his good foot. The pain in his leg was bad today; perversely, that made him glad. He deserved the raw twinges in his knee joint. He stared out of the window, his position on the top floor of the lodge giving him an amazing view out over

17

the front of the house and beyond to the wild lands of the estate. His mind roved back to his conversation earlier with his father. The telephone line from the States was as clear as if Donal MacDonald was in the neighbouring room.

'Your flight home's booked, Cal. I've been more than generous, letting you go over to that godforsaken place to lick your wounds and sulk. It's time to come back. What am I paying you for? The business needs you.'

There was no enquiry after his wellbeing or state of mind. He didn't expect that from the old man. Since when did Donal care about his sons' emotional health? He'd left that kind of thing to their mother. And since she was too busy playing the social scene in New York, it had been left to a succession of nannies to try to bring up two rowdy boys. Cal barely spoke to his mother these days.

'I'm not coming home yet.' Cal kept his voice neutral. Donal's temper was legendary and easily kindled into life. 'A few more weeks, then I'll take that flight.' He put the phone down on his father's bluster, and didn't answer when it immediately rang and rang.

His own temper had risen in response to Donal's imperious demands. He was damn sure he wasn't going back until he was ready. He'd been gone two months, and that wasn't enough. He needed more time. When he did return, he wanted to be the same man that had left. Not a figure of pity with his damaged leg, nor fuel for more media interest. He sighed in exasperation and stared out through the glass.

Down below, on the circular paved entrance, he saw a slim figure with a rucksack walking determinedly away from the house. It was the woman he'd met earlier in the stables. He felt a twinge of guilt. He hadn't acted well towards her. The anger with his father had simmered and overflowed into his conversation with her. Kinash most likely wouldn't have freaked if she stroked him. He was highly strung, but acted out infrequently.

He almost smiled. She'd squared up to him when he shouted at her. It reminded him of his terrier left at home in the States, small but ferociously courageous when faced with larger creatures. There had been a momentary admiration for her. And a touch of something else, if he was honest. She had a pretty enough face, framed by shoulder-length pale yellow hair. Her large grey eyes were too expressive; she'd be useless at a game of poker. Yet, despite her ordinariness, he'd felt a little shoot of adrenaline when he watched her soft, full mouth as she spoke. A tiny curl of desire.

Cal gave a short, harsh laugh. He wasn't going to go there. There was no way he was getting involved with another woman, however desirable he found her. And the young woman striding down the long Invermalloch driveway was nothing special to look at. He'd had his pick of beauties in the

States, and look where that had got him. Now all he wanted was to hide out and keep to himself until he was ready to return.

'Cal?' Helen put her head round the door. 'Have you got a moment?'

'What's the matter?' Cal was fond of Helen. She was the MacDonalds' point of contact for their Scottish property, and did an excellent job of it.

'I'm a little worried about Lara, the girl who was here. I didn't give her a job, and she's gone. She told me she had a place to stay tonight but I'm not sure that's true.'

'She'll get a place in the village.'

'I don't think so. The Givens' bed and breakfast is full for the Murray wedding, and so is the guest house. There isn't anywhere else, I've just checked.'

Trust Helen to do so. She was too kind-hearted. Cal didn't want to get involved. Surely this Lara was an adult and could manage by herself. But Helen was looking at him steadily.

'Cal?'

He gave an exasperated sigh.

'Very well, I'll go get her. You can organise a room for her overnight. Just make sure it's far away from my suite. I don't want to be disturbed.'

He glimpsed Helen's smile as he went past, tight-lipped. He'd go and pick the damn girl up, and if he was lucky he needn't see her again that evening — or in the morning, either. He'd make sure to tell Helen she was to be on her way early tomorrow.

2

Lara was trudging through an increasingly heavy rain shower when the battered Land Rover pulled up beside her. The window was rolled down and Cal's frowning face appeared.

'Get in.'

The passenger door was flung open.

'I don't need a lift,' Lara said. Did he have to be so bossy? Her feet ached and there was an freezing trickle of water down the back of her neck, but she wasn't going to humbly obey him at the snap of his fingers.

'Get in, please.'

'You have a problem with that word, don't you?' Lara said sharply.

He surprised them both with his laugh. It lit up his face, making it at once younger and, if it were possible, even more deliciously handsome. Lara thought of summer skies instead of icy

Scottish lochs in the blue of his gaze.

'Please let me give you a lift. Helen insists you stay the night at Invermalloch.'

So he could be charming when he wished to be. His blue eyes held a mute appeal and he was even smiling just a little. Lara softened. She went round the back of the vehicle and slid into the passenger seat. Her rucksack was beyond heavy now, soaked in the rainwater. She heaved it in between her feet.

'I could've got a bed in the village,' she remarked, as he expertly turned the Land Rover back the way he'd come.

'No, you couldn't. Helen tells me they're all booked out for a wedding party.'

'Oh.' Again, she didn't know what to say for a moment. He had a strange effect on her. Unsettling. She was so close to him in the front seat that she could feel his body warmth emanating. The tiny hairs on her forearms rose up in awareness.

'How does Helen know so much?' For want of something else to say, and to break the oddly comforting silence between them.

He glanced over at her and quickly back at the road. The windscreen wipers were working hard to clear the streams of water. The side windows were misting up, making the inside of the vehicle seem smaller, and Cal closer to her. Lara shifted over to her side. He frowned, and the laugh might never have happened.

'Helen's from a local family. She works for my family here at Invermalloch, and keeps us updated in New York with what's happening on the estate.'

So he was from New York. That explained the accent, a mingling of East coast America and Highland Scotland. A mixture that was alluring. Another icy drip slid down the inside of her shirt, and she was glad of the shock of it. She didn't want to think about the Laird of Invermalloch. Not one little bit. She'd stay the night and be out of there fast in the morning. If she was lucky, she needn't cross paths with him again.

'Are you on holiday?' she asked, then mentally kicked herself. He was the Laird of this land. Probably lairds had to do their fair share of turning up to inspect their properties. What did she know?

'No.'

It was his turn to give a one-word answer. Well, that was fine. She didn't really care. Okay, she was a tiny bit curious about him, but she'd control that. Besides, tomorrow she'd be far north of here.

* * *

The room she was shown to by the housekeeper was large, sparsely furnished with dark, old walnut wardrobes and a matching chest of drawers. With a muttered instruction to shout if she needed anything, the taciturn old woman left. Lara sat on the end of the bed, feeling cold and damp. The rain had soaked into her jacket and canvas boots, and her hair was wet to the scalp. Her belongings looked small and forlorn in the middle of the floor. The bed was covered in an old-fashioned quilt and crocheted pink blanket, and the housekeeper had laid out three soft, thick white towels for her, which looked brand new. Lara took the top one gratefully and decided to take a hot shower.

She went quietly out of the room with the towel and a change of clothes clutched to her. Now, where would the shower room be? She was on the middle storey of the house and on a long, narrow corridor with many doors leading off it. She saw the landing and the polished wooden banister of the staircase she'd followed the house-keeper up. In the distance downstairs she heard voices and a woman's laughter. Where she stood, there was nothing but the creak of old wood and a beam of dancing dust motes now the sun had deigned to show its weak evening light. She remembered reading that, up here in the Highlands in the summer, it never really got dark until midnight.

She tiptoed along, hoping for an open door or a sign to the bathroom. Her vision fixed to her left and, looking for clues, she walked bang into a solid shape. Or, rather, a solid, muscular chest. She put her arms out to push back and looked up straight into Cal's face. There was a flicker of amusement before his customary scowl was put in place.

'Sorry, I didn't see you. I was looking for the shower.' Lara wasn't cold any more. The heat rising in her skin was warming her. Her fingertips were still touching his chest and she dropped her hands abruptly. They tingled with the feel of his rough cotton shirt. She smelt soap and clean hair. He'd had a shower, then. An unbidden image of his muscled body in the shower made her flush even more. What was the matter with her? Honestly, couldn't she simply be polite and pleasant to her host?

'Second door along.' Cal's voice was rough, as if he had a cold coming on.

She followed his gaze. *Sheesh*. Her fresh set of underwear had fallen to the floor. They lay in all their silken skimpy glory on the carpet. She grabbed them and stuffed them in with the other change of clothes.

'Right,' Lara said, pointing at the bathroom door and nodding conversationally, 'I'll go and have a shower then.' *Stupid. Stupid.*

'Dinner's at seven. If you'd like to join us.' Said stiffly, as if he hoped she'd refuse.

He didn't know her. She liked a challenge. Never stepped down from one. *Only once.* She'd run away from Jason and from her wedding. That challenge was too overwhelming and unforgiveable.

'I'd love to join you. Seven it is,' she said brightly.

She made herself pass him casually,

and even managed to hum a little tune as she shut the bathroom door. Once it was locked, she let out a long puff of breath.

*   *   *

The dining room at Invermalloch Lodge was like a scene from an old film, Lara decided. The table was dark oak, and long enough to seat ten people. The curtains draped against the winter evening were of sombre olive velvet, and looked like they were possibly of original Victorian vintage. As Lara hesitantly went in, the dour housekeeper was serving up soup to the three people seated there. Lara's glance went instinctively to Cal at the head of the table. He hadn't noticed her presence yet, and his face was as brooding as the gloomy backdrop. To his left sat Helen. She was wearing a blue frock and had clearly dressed for dinner, which made Lara glad she'd also made an effort with her own limited wardrobe. To Cal's right was an older man with white hair and a bushy moustache. He looked more like a Highland Laird than Cal, Lara thought with amusement.

Cal looked up and saw her. He smiled politely and indicated for her to join them. She threw him a quick glance as she sat beside Helen. He'd lost the dark expression and looked marginally happier. She wondered what it was that bothered him so. Helen's words came back to her, from the lift in her car. What was it she'd said? *He's not well, poor soul.* Apart from a limp, he looked physically strong and broad-shouldered. Was Helen talking about his leg, or was there something more serious wrong with him?

'Lara, you've met Helen. This is Bob Stanton, Invermalloch's excellent estate manager,' Cal said.

Bob Stanton inclined his head in a friendly greeting. 'I hear you're looking for a post as wildlife ranger here. It's an interesting idea. Not a job we've had here before.'

'I don't know if you need one,' Lara said awkwardly. 'I'm heading north tomorrow to see if there are any opportunities.'

'We haven't ruled it out, have we Helen?' Cal said.

'I think we agreed I'd discuss it with you and give Lara an answer tomorrow,' Helen replied, with a smile.

'Excellent,' he said, turning his piercing blue eyes on Lara. 'That gives me time to find out all about what a ranger does.'

Lara's stomach did a little flip. Spending time with Cal MacDonald sounded good but unnerving. Why did he have this physical effect on her? He certainly wasn't relaxing company. In fact, he was the opposite. When she was near him, her whole body seemed to tighten up and she was hyper-aware of him. She hadn't ever felt this with another man. Certainly not with Jason. She'd known him forever, and there had been a soft, comfortable ease between them — of familiarity, and of what she'd imagined to be a deep love.

Lara shut her eyes tightly for a moment. She couldn't bear to think about Jason. Not tonight. She opened them to find Cal's gaze fixed on her. Then he looked away, as if faintly annoyed, and started speaking to Bob about the estate.

Lara felt herself relax. The game soup was delicious, and the room was warm from a large open log fire and the lit candles on the table. The housekeeper served up generous quantities of stew and vegetables and the conversation flowed, most of it concentrated on the affairs of the estate. She sensed a great affection in all three of them for the place they lived and worked on. She noted Cal's courtesy to his staff, too. He listened well to Bob's advice on the estate management and to Helen's suggestions regarding the house. When the dessert, a lemon sherbet, was finished, Bob and

Helen made their excuses.

'Thanks for dinner, Cal,' Bob said. 'I'd better head off; got to rise at five, and I need my beauty sleep.'

'Me too,' Helen agreed. 'I don't have to get up at quite such an awful hour, but I'm really tired tonight. It was lovely to get to know you better, Lara, and I'll see you in the morning for a chat.'

There was a silence between Lara and Cal when the other two had gone. A log sparked in the fire, and the coals rattled as the ash crumbled down the grate.

'They're both very nice,' Lara said, wanting to break the strange atmosphere and lift the darkness that shadowed his face again.

'Yes, and very dedicated to Invermalloch,' he answered; she was relieved to see him make an effort to converse.

Hoping to keep him interested, and stop him dwelling on whatever it was that haunted his thoughts, she went on brightly, 'So, you live in America. Do you come over here regularly? It's quite a long journey from New York.'

'This is my first visit in a long while,' he admitted, lifting the bottle the housekeeper had left and pouring two glasses of ruby-coloured wine. 'But I spent all my boyhood summers here, running wild. My grandparents owned the estate in those days, and had no idea what to do with my brother and me. It was a kid's paradise.'

Lara imagined a young Cal racing through the heather and fishing in the streams. There must have been a freedom in his youth, and happiness. So what had happened to change the boy into the serious adult man?

'Sounds great, but your parents must've missed you.' Lara sipped the wine and enjoyed the way the candle-light shone through the glass. Despite the size of the room, there was a cosy intimacy to their conversation. The glow of the candles cast a circle of light around them and the rest of the room was shadowed and unnecessary.

He gave a bitter chuckle. 'They didn't miss us one bit. We were shipped off to Scotland each summer to give them space. My father is a businessman, and a good one, but he's a workaholic. And my mother is a New York socialite. Neither of them wanted to be hampered by two lively boys who were, quite frankly, out of control. It was left to my grandparents to try to instil some sense into us.'

Lara tried to imagine her own parents not wanting her or Malorie. It was impossible. She'd been surrounded by a loving family her whole life. Even as an adult, her mother liked to phone and keep in touch with what she was doing and how she was feeling. Her father was a quiet, calming and loving influence on both daughters and his wife. She felt suddenly sorry for Cal. He was a man who appeared to have it all. Effortless good looks, charm and incredible wealth. Yet he was missing what Lara considered essential to a happy life. Her heart went out to him.

If she'd known him better, she'd have leaned forward and hugged him close.

And where would that lead? She'd barely touched him with her fingertips earlier and they'd burned with the contact. Much safer to keep her distance. Besides, she would be gone tomorrow. Any attraction she had was a mere animal instinct, soon forgotten in her new life in the north.

Cal was annoyed at himself. He didn't want to think about women, or be attracted to another one, after Anthea. Yet Lara's large grey and expressive eyes were getting to him. He'd even worried momentarily about her when she squeezed them shut during dinner. When she opened them again, there was a pain in them that she quickly hid. Now those same eyes were shimmering with pity for him, and he wished he hadn't mentioned his child-hood. The thing was, he had tried to speak about it objectively. And he and Garrett had had marvellous summers here at Invermalloch with all the heady freedom two kids could need. But he never could describe his parents without some bitterness seeping through, however much he wanted to let it all go. Somehow, it was all caught up with his relationship with Anthea, and the accident, and he'd put all of it in a mental iron box and locked it up.

More to stop Lara's empathy than out of curiosity, Cal asked her about her suggested post. 'Persuade me we need a ranger,' he said, refilling the wine glasses.

'You've got an awful lot of land here, and there are probably priority habitats and species that need recording and surveyed. I can do that, and I can also bring you in some revenue by taking groups out to see the wildlife, boosting the area's green tourism.'

'Wow, that's a sales pitch. Did you practise that before coming down here this evening?'

Was he teasing her? Did the Laird of Invermalloch actually lighten up and make a joke?

'Actually, yes, I did. It's a prepared answer,' Lara grinned. 'Did you like it?'

'I do like it.'

The way he was looking at her, the deep timbre of his voice, sent a little sliver of delight up her spine. But maybe she was imagining it because then he sounded quite normal, quite the prospective employer, when he asked:

'What equipment would you need?'

'Not a huge lot. I'd need pond dipping nets and trays, maybe some magnifying glasses and binoculars.'

There was such enthusiasm in her voice, he felt infected by it. Her face shone with it and became almost beautiful. He'd called her ordinary to himself, but she didn't look it now. Her cheeks were flushed, her eyes sparkled and her mouth was softly inviting. She teased at her lower lip with perfect white teeth as she waited for his answer. His body stirred unwillingly. What would she do if he leaned forward and tasted her lips with his? Most likely she'd give him a slap for his impudence. He'd already tangled with her terrier-like stubbornness.

'Cal?'

Even his name on her tongue sounded good. Cal pushed his wine glass away. He'd drunk too much, that was it.

'Let me think on it overnight,' he said abruptly. He pushed his chair back to indicate the evening was finished, and tried to ignore the hurt surprise in her face at his change of mood.

★　★　★

Lara lay in bed with all the covers pulled up over her, and still felt cold. Outside the window, an owl was hunting, its mournful hoot loud and haunting. She thought of all the tiny creatures scurrying for cover in the grass as its wings swept the moors. She thought of Cal and his strange, abrupt ending to the evening just as she was beginning to enjoy his company. And there was the danger. She didn't want to enjoy being with him. It couldn't end well. Thank goodness she was leaving in a few hours' time.

She drifted into a restless sleep sewn through with patches of dreams where she and Jason were walking up a long, long aisle. She was wearing her beautiful wedding dress, that Malorie had helped her pick, and her long veil covered her face. She was so happy until they reached the altar and there was a woman standing there. She turned and tore the veil from Lara's face. It was Kate, her best friend. In the dream, Kate grabbed Jason and they were running, running and Lara couldn't keep up. She screamed and woke up. Her limbs were tangled in the bedsheets and her heart was pounding. Her body felt clammy and she sat up, letting the nightmare fade away.

Lara slid her feet out of bed onto the cold floor. She was all of a sudden desperately thirsty and blamed the two glasses of wine she'd drunk earlier. No doubt they had caused her terrible dreams too. She'd run along to the kitchen downstairs and get herself a drink of water.

Clad only in her nightie, for lack of a robe, she pushed open her bedroom door and went out as quietly as possible. She didn't want to wake anyone. She wasn't sure how many people had rooms in the lodge. Did Helen go home to the village? Did the housekeeper live in? She didn't know, and didn't want to find out tonight.

She tried to remember the layout of the downstairs. She could find the dining room okay, and she was pretty sure the kitchen wasn't far from it. That made sense. The servants in the past wouldn't have had to ferry food and porcelain too far. She passed the dining room and the smoky scent of the banked-up fire. Then she went across the hall and into the darkness of the kitchen.

Not daring to put on a light for fear of discovery, she fumbled her way into the room. Then a sixth sense made her freeze. There was someone there. Her skin bristled with the knowledge. The moon shone through the old glass windows; she saw the outline of a tall man and gave a small, involuntary scream.

He stepped forward and she saw it was Cal.

'You scared me,' Lara hissed, fear turning to irritation at herself and at him for causing it.

'I'm simply getting a glass of water from my own kitchen,' he retorted. 'What about you?'

She heard the mild emphasis on the word 'own' and blushed. Lucky it was dark, so he didn't see it. She felt foolish. And very conscious of the thin nightie she was wearing. She hugged her arms around her and tried not to stare at his bare chest. He was clad only in shorts, and she saw the outline of strongly muscled thighs in the thin, silvery light as the clouds shifted.

'A glass of water, please,' she

mumbled. 'I couldn't sleep.'

'Neither could I. Too much wine for both of us tonight.' There was a touch of humour in his voice, she noted with relief.

He turned on the tap, poured a glass of water and handed it to her. Their fingers touched briefly, and she pulled away so fast the glass slopped.

'Thanks.' She drank it down with speed, needing to get away, to put some distance between her and the Laird of Invermalloch.

As she ran back upstairs to the safety of her bedroom, Lara knew she could do nothing about it. She was most definitely *very* attracted to Cal Mac-Donald.

3

'This is the cottage. I hope it's okay for you; it's quite old and in need of some renovation,' Helen said, unlocking the front door.

Lara ducked under a fringe of cobwebs and followed her inside. She still couldn't believe she had the job. Cal had spoken to Helen, and not only did she have a whole season's employment right up to autumn, she had an advance on her wages — which was a relief. The job came with an estate cottage rent-free, Helen had told her. Cal's orders, she'd added, when Lara offered once more to pay for its use.

'It's marvellous, thanks.'

The cottage was no more than four rooms on one level. There was a living room, a kitchen, one bedroom at the back and a tiny bathroom. The rooms were bare and dusty, with the minimum of furniture, but Lara didn't care. She already had a plan to sweep and wash the floors, and to polish up the wood and wipe the windows clear.

'I'll leave you to get settled in,' Helen said doubtfully. 'Are you sure you don't want a hand with the scrubbing? I could send one of the stable girls over.'

'No, really, I'm looking forward to sorting it out,' Lara said, laughing. 'I'm excited by its potential.' And glad not to have to spend a second night in the huge Invermalloch Lodge. A vision of Cal half-naked and rumpled with sleep flashed before her eyes. No, there was danger in being too close to him. Far better to be in this ramshackle little house.

'I'll be curious to see it when it's ready.' Helen smiled. 'Good luck. Remember, Cal doesn't need you to start working right away. In a day or two will be fine.'

'I really have landed on my feet.' Lara smiled back. 'It's my dream job.'

'I must admit, I was surprised when

Cal told me he wanted to take you on. But I'm glad. It's good he's taking a more active interest in the estate. Invermalloch needs a bit of loving attention from its owner.'

'Is he staying on here long-term?'

'I couldn't say.' Helen turned away, clearly unwilling to say more. She was loyal to Cal, that was evident.

When she'd gone, Lara took a moment to enjoy having her own space. The view from the grimy window was amazing. It looked right out over the heather moors and a patch of thin white birch trees to the foothills of the nearby mountains. A stony track led from the cottage door into the distance, between the trees and up the grassy slopes of the nearest hill.

She took the pail and mop that Helen had given her, ran lukewarm water from the tap, and added a generous gloop of washing liquid. There was heating and electricity in the cottage, but she'd been warned that the heating system could be intermittent and the electrics were ancient. She didn't care. It was good of Cal to give her the job and a place to stay. She knew there were other estate cottages where the stable hands lived, and that Bob Stanton had the largest house — visible from the lodge, with a neatly tended garden, a garage and car parking. She pulled a wry grin. There was no chance of a garden round this cottage. The wilderness grew right up to her front doorstep. If she was here long enough, she could wrest a flowerbed from it. But she was only here for two to three months tops. It would have to do.

She started with the bare floorboards of the living room and washed them down, working hard with the mop and warming up with the exercise. She ran through lists in her head as she scrubbed. The advance wages would pay for clothes. She'd need thick jeans or cotton trousers, new trainers, and a few tees and fleeces. There was no glamour required for rangering. It was all about protection from the cold and dirt and elements.

She leaned on the mop handle for a breath. With satisfaction, she saw the floorboards were clean and the grain of the wood now shone through. She decided she should phone home and get Malorie to send up some belongings. There was a lamp she owned that would look great in the nook on the wide stone windowsill. Then there was her silver coffee maker, which she swore made the best coffee ever. She looked about, glad of an excuse for a break, mentally listing a few more items she couldn't live without.

There was an old Bakelite phone in the kitchen. Surprisingly, it was connected. She wiped it free of dust and rang the number.

Malorie answered, sounding both happy to hear her and tetchy with her for not getting in touch sooner.

'Mum and Dad are really worried about you. It's selfish of you, Lara. You could've got to a phone sooner.'

'I'm sorry,' Lara said, feeling the

usual guilty rush she got when she spoke with her sister. 'I didn't want to call until I knew where I'd ended up. I've got a job and a place to stay, so please tell the parents I'm fine.'

There was a pause at the other end of the line, and she heard nothing but scratchy air until Malorie spoke again.

'You should phone them yourself, you know, but I'm going round there tonight with Tom so I'll let them know.'

Malorie, a single mum to three-year-old-Tom, lived near the elder Hayneses. She kept an eye on them, and they helped her out with their much-loved grandson. It was a mutually contented arrangement.

'Where are you, anyway?' Malorie asked with an audible sigh.

It was odd, the way family relationships played out in ever-repeating patterns, Lara mused. Malorie was the older sister and had always been protective of Lara. And, as the younger sister, Lara had got away with being impetuous and stubborn and following her own dictates. But she loved her parents and Malorie, and didn't want to cause them hurt or worry. Inevitably, whatever she did, she felt guilty for doing it. But this time she'd excelled herself. She'd run away from her flat, her fiancé and her life without a thought of anyone else, caught up in her own world of misery.

'I'm in the Scottish Highlands,' she said. 'It's very beautiful up here, but rather intimidating on a grand scale. I've got a job as a wildlife ranger for the season. I'm okay. Really.'

Another pause. 'What about Jason? He's distraught. He wants to phone you. Can I tell him you'll listen to what he has to say?'

Lara's knuckles tightened white on the phone cord. *Distraught.* How dare he! When he was the one who'd caused all this in the first place.

'How can you ask that of me?' Her voice shook as she answered Malorie. She felt sick.

'It wasn't all his fault, Lara. You know that. Don't be your usual stubborn self. Bend a little, like everyone else has to.'

'Like you did with Finn when he left you?'

It was a low body punch, but Lara didn't care. She felt again the anguish of the past few weeks.

'That was different . . . Don't change the subject. This isn't about my love life or lack of it, it's about your future. You and Jason. You're so good together, so right for each other. I can't believe you're going to give him up without fighting for him.'

The air drained out of Lara's lungs, and she was left deflated. A great weariness crept over her.

'How's Kate?' she made herself ask, tasting a sourness in her mouth like an unripe apple.

'She's sorry too. Look, Lara . . . I know it's a mess. But promise me you'll think about it. And let Jason call you. He wants you back.'

*　*　*

Cal pushed his laptop away with an angry sigh, and stood up. Moving across the room, he stared out of the window, not seeing the view. He couldn't concentrate on his work, was antsy today. He thought to saddle up Kinash and test his leg by a long ride through the glen. But that reminded of him of the first time he'd seen Lara, and that just brought his thoughts back to how she'd looked last night. Did she realise how thin that nightie was? In the moonlight every curve and dip was visible. She had a slender waist, and the outline of her breasts ... His body hardened. Dammit!

Okay, he was a normal male with the usual array of instincts when it came to pretty women. That didn't mean he had to take it any further. It was his own fault for telling Helen to give Lara a job and a cottage for the summer. He didn't want to delve deeper into his own motivations about that.

With a muttered oath, Cal went back to his chair and opened the laptop again. He might not be at the helm of the business in the family's New York offices, but he could work remotely here at Invermalloch. It would keep his father off his back; and mean, too, that when he finally returned home, he'd still have his finger on the pulse.

The phone rang just as he was beginning to make sense of the first spreadsheet.

'Hey Cal, whaddya up to?' A lazily warm greeting from his younger brother.

'Garrett, it's good to hear from you.' *And unlikely*, Cal added silently. His brother wasn't one for casual telephone chats. There had to be another reason for the call. 'Did Dad put you up to this?'

'Dad? No, no, buddy, I'm missing you; that's why I'm calling. When ya comin' home?'

In spite of their dual nationality and

upbringing, Garrett was very much an all-American guy. He'd chosen that path and loved that lifestyle. Cal had, too — until the accident. Now, it felt different. *He* was different.

'A few weeks, like I told Dad,' Cal said patiently.

'How's the leg?'

'It's better. Almost no pain these days. How are you?' Changing the subject neatly. He was fed up thinking about himself and his leg, and how he'd got the break in the first place.

'I'm good. New car, new girl, parties . . . You're missing out, and I'm missing my party pardner.'

The MacDonald brothers. Notorious for both the wild parties they held, and the parties they attended. The 'work hard and play harder' ethic that Donal MacDonald had encouraged in them. The old man had been just as wild in his day.

Cal shook his head. 'I'd only be holding you back if I was there.' The truth was, he'd lost the taste for it.

Somewhere along the way, even before the accident, he was jaded with his life. Anthea's constant needs for stimulation and material wealth had finally revolted him. Which was completely unfair of him, since that was what he'd offered her at first. He'd wanted her on those terms, and then, somehow, it wasn't enough. He'd tried to explain it to her. That day, before the accident.

'Cal . . . Cal? You still there?' Garrett's voice loud in the receiver.

'Yeah, I'm here.' But only just, as the remembered sound of the belching fire echoed in his head.

'So, what's with the Highland hideout, man? Seriously, you can't be enjoying it, can you?' Garrett sounded disbelieving over the miles of transatlantic cabling.

Cal laughed. 'Actually, I am. It's brought back all sorts of memories from when we were kids here. You should come over and stay. There's a freedom here, Garrett, which we don't have in New York.'

'No way. I love you, brother, but that's an ask too far. Can you imagine me out in the wilderness with no restaurants and no gorgeous girls?'

Cal couldn't. Garrett was very much a city dweller now he was grown. The young lad that had followed Cal through some hair-raising escapades at Invermalloch had gone. But he was wrong about the lack of gorgeous girls, Cal thought. If he sent a photo of Lara to Garrett, he wouldn't be surprised if his brother was on the next flight out. And why that should make his guts clench, he didn't know. Anyway, it wasn't happening. He needn't mention his newest employee at all.

'I gotta go,' Garrett said. 'I'll catch ya later, yeah?'

Cal said his goodbyes and put the receiver down. It was morning over on the Eastern seaboard, and he knew Garrett was on his way out to spend another day enjoying himself — to be followed by a night of partying high and long, then crashing wherever he ended up. He didn't need to work, courtesy of their mother's family's trust fund. It was the worst decision their parents had made, Cal believed. For complicated legal reasons to do with his maternal grandfather, Cal didn't have the same luxury of a trust to depend on. But he was glad of it. Having to work had kept the world sane for him. Up until recently, the two sides of his life had balanced — work and play. Then it had all come apart.

Kinash whinnied a welcome, thrusting his hairy nose into Cal's face. He stroked the horse's powerful neck and talked to him in a low, soothing tone. One of the stable hands saddled and bridled the big animal, and Cal swung himself up, waiting for the pain to hit his leg. It was mild discomfort rather than the stabbing fire that he had got used to. He was on the mend for sure. His leg was his calendar, a guide to how long he'd stay here. Once it was fully healed, he'd be going back to America. Gauging it by today, he only had a few weeks left at Invermalloch at most.

He guided Kinash at a canter out of the cobbled stableyard, too fast for him and for the horse. His intention was to head for the horizon and the steeply rising hills so he could blast his restlessness out in the sharp, whistling air. Instead, he found himself circling round the buildings and out across a short, heathery field to a single white cottage tucked amongst the rushy grasses. He got down, wincing as his knee jarred, and tied the reins round the nearest birch trunk. It would be a courtesy to call on her. Boss to new employee, just to ask if she was settling in okay.

Now that he'd justified it, Cal raised his hand to knock on the cottage door. Behind him, Kinash rasped at the tussocks, feeding contentedly.

The door opened abruptly and Lara appeared, lugging a full bucket of grey water. She put it down heavily at the sight of him.

'Are you checking up on me?' she said, with a tight smile, as if to show she was joking; still, it came over as if she was annoyed with him.

Cal scanned her expression. Her face was pinched and unhappy. He wondered what had happened to make it so. He hoped it wasn't a reaction to their accidental meeting last night in the lodge kitchen. But then, he couldn't think why she'd be so bothered about that. Nothing had happened, except an exchange of embarrassment and a glass of water.

'Is everything okay?' he asked, noticing how her lips thinned and she stared into the bucket with great intensity.

She glanced up at him then and seemed to make an effort to relax her features. The pinched look vanished; and, although she was still pale, her prettiness returned. Not that he was focusing on that, he reminded himself.

'Yes, thanks. I'm very grateful for the use of the cottage. I've been cleaning out, as you can see from the colour of the water.'

So, whatever was bothering her, she wasn't going to share. Why should she? They didn't know each other well enough for confidences. He shrugged mentally. It wasn't any of his business.

'Can I come in?' Cal ducked his head under the low entrance when she nodded her agreement. 'This brings back old memories.'

'Did you know this place as a boy?' Lara leaned on the ancient sideboard to look up at him curiously.

'Yes, my grandparents allowed us to use the cottage as a den. There was no one living here in those days; it was standing empty. Lots of good times for me and my brother. It was variously a fort or a castle or a thieves' getaway place.'

She brushed her pale blonde hair back from her face, leaving a dusty streak on her cheekbone. He had an impulse to lean over and wipe it away. How would her skin feel? Soft and delicate and warm. He looked away.

'Does your brother ever visit here now?'

'No.' His answer was terse. He regretted it when she turned from him. But he'd no desire to explain his family further.

'Okaaay . . . ' She drew the word out, making it clearly a hint for him to go.

He didn't know why he'd come by. Certainly not to make conversation. He'd blown that with his monosyllabic answer to her innocuous question. Outside, he heard the jangle of the metal harness. Kinash was getting impatient. He should go. So why was he reluctant to do so?

Helpfully, he reached for the bucket handle. He'd pour out the heavy, dirty water for her before he went. Unfortunately, she went for it at the same moment, and they collided. He felt the softness of her hair against his cheek and smelt a fragrance of sweet flowers. He steadied her, lifting her upright, and his hands closed on her waist to do so.

Her body warmth soaked into his fingers, leaving them heated and tingling. Her face was close to his for just a moment, and his mouth ached to press onto hers. Then she pushed him firmly from her. She was breathing fast, her chest rising and falling. She wasn't pale now. There was bright colour staining her cheeks, and her large, grey eyes were darkly luminous.

He didn't trust himself to say anything. He strode quickly to Kinash and swung up to the saddle. He turned the animal with a jerk of the reins and urged him to a gallop. Away from his childhood cottage. Away from Lara Haynes.

He slowed the horse once he'd put a distance between them. His leg ached. But not as much as other body parts. God, what was wrong with him? Whenever he was close to her, his body reacted instinctively. There was a raw physical magnetism that drew him to her. He didn't understand it. She wasn't a New York beauty. She was an ordinary girl with a prettiness like thousands of others.

Cal frowned at the mountains ahead of him. Then he pressed his heels to Kinash's flanks and the horse obediently trotted on. He might find Lara attractively compelling, but that didn't mean he had to like it. After his relationship with Anthea, he certainly wasn't ready to date another woman — even one who appeared to be the opposite of his ex-fiancée.

4

Lara was on fire. Where his hands had cupped her waist, there was a blaze along her nerve endings. She'd been so close to him that she'd seen the flecks of grey in his crystal-blue eyes. Those eyes had darkened when their lips almost met. It was as if that moment of their collision had slowed right down, so that she saw and felt every detail of their accidental embrace. It was crazy. She didn't know him, but her body felt like it did. Pure animal attraction, she decided, as she took the offending bucket and poured out the dirty water under the trees. It had nothing to do with liking or loving, and so she could ignore it. She *would* ignore it.

Biting down on the niggling thought that Cal MacDonald wasn't a man to be easily forgotten, Lara kept cleaning. She wanted the cottage to be a real home, however temporary. The hard work took her mind off a tautly-muscled body, deep blue gaze and midnight-thick hair.

In a cupboard, she found old blankets and cushions. Inspecting them, she found they were still in good condition, if a little faded from usage. She draped a green tartan blanket over the small sofa in the living room, and added three cushions in shades of olive and forest. Satisfied, she sat on the sofa to test it. It was comfortable and she lay back, pulling her feet up and using one cushion for a pillow.

He wants you back. Malorie's words about Jason came into her head. He had a real cheek, telling her sister that and knowing Malorie would pass it on to Lara. As if she'd take him back after what he had done. He and Kate. Yet wasn't a part of her glad Jason still cared? A little flare of hope had raised up when Malorie told her about him. He and Kate were no longer together. Maybe it really had been pre-wedding nerves, as Jason had pleaded.

Lara sighed and sat up. She didn't know what to think any more. Which was why she'd escaped up here to the Highlands. She wanted space to think it all through. Maybe, at the end of the summer, she'd go back to Devon. Back to Jason. She didn't know what she was going to do. One thing was for certain, she wasn't going to let Malorie and Jason make the decision for her.

Lara decided she'd let Malorie tell Jason she'd accept his call. But that didn't mean she was softening towards him. Pleased with that decision, she scooted off the low sofa and headed for the kitchen to make coffee. She might not have her coffee machine yet, but there was an old pan and strainer in the cupboard that would do in the meantime, and Helen had thoughtfully left her a bag of groceries as a starter kit.

She rummaged in the plastic bag and found a carton of ground filter coffee. She boiled up water that rattled cold and clear from the tap as if coming directly from the stream outside. Maybe it did.

She was adding spoonfuls of coffee when she heard the noise of hooves. It was hours since Cal had ridden off on Kinash. Surely they couldn't still be riding? She left the pan simmering, and went to the front of the cottage.

The door was open as she had left it to let the fresh summer air in to freshen the house. Now she saw it was Cal. He slid from the horse's back as if exhausted. There was foam on Kinash's flanks and his nostrils flared. Cal limped towards her, his face grey.

Lara ran to him, and put her shoulder under his arm to prop him up.

'Are you alright? What happened?' she said as they staggered together into the living room.

He waited until he was half-lying on her sofa before he answered.

'I didn't mean to bother you. I was stupid. I rode too far, and I've tired Kinash and myself out.' He groaned as he moved his leg.

'Is your leg hurt?' she asked quickly, moving to his side.

'No more than usual. I'll be fine if I can rest here for a few minutes.' He lay his head back onto the cushion Lara had been using. It gave her an odd little feeling to see his dark hair where hers had been so recently. It seemed . . . intimate.

'Of course,' she said hastily, trying to prevent her thoughts going astray. 'Can I offer you a coffee?'

'Is that what I smell burning in the back?' Cal's mouth twisted in a half smile while he rubbed at his knee.

'Oh!' Lara leapt up and ran to save the coffee pan.

She threw the stewed mess down the sink hole and made a fresh brew. It gave her five minutes' grace while she came to terms with the fact that Cal was back in her house and lying on her makeshift bed. When she used it again, she'd think of the mould of his body there . . .

Stop it right now. The poor man

needed her. He had a sore leg and a weary horse, and he'd clearly overdone his riding for the day. She had to stop thinking sexy thoughts about him.

Besides, how did he see her? Probably as just another seasonal employee. He was the Laird of this vast acreage of land. And she was . . . what? A girl who had lost her job and her fiancé and her self-belief. Hardly an attractive prospect for a man who could presumably pick and choose from the best.

Why was she even thinking that way? Lara gave herself a mental kick. She wasn't on the lookout for a replacement for Jason. She was never going to trust another man the way she had him. And he'd caused her trust to be ripped apart. That told her something. She was better keeping her heart safely behind the wall she'd built around it.

She poured the coffee into two large mugs and took them through to the living room. Cal was lying back on the sofa, his long legs stretched out over the end of it. He sat up carefully and grinned when he saw her. Lara's heart did a little flip.

'How's your leg now?' she asked with concern.

'Better for the rest. Thanks for taking me in.'

'I could hardly refuse to let you enter your own property,' she said tartly.

He frowned. 'Hey, while you rent it, consider the cottage yours. I don't have any rights over it, and I wouldn't come in without your permission.'

'I was sort of joking,' Lara said. 'Of course I'd let you in to rest your leg.' He was too serious for his own good. Was he always this way? She could hardly imagine him at a social event, being lively and conversational.

He lifted the mug and drank. She got a view of the strong column of his neck, and of his Adam's apple moving as the coffee went down. There was a dark shadow of bristle on his jaw. Her stomach clenched. He was powerfully male, and suddenly the small room seemed even smaller.

She dropped her gaze as he put the mug down. The atmosphere was thick like smoke. She had an impulse to jump up, to run, to be anywhere but so close to Cal MacDonald that her fingers could touch him without effort.

'You were upset earlier.' It was a statement, not a question.

It broke the spell. Almost with relief, Lara found herself nodding.

His blue eyes sought hers. 'What was wrong?'

He looked like he genuinely cared. Which couldn't be true. He hardly knew her, and she simply worked for him. Hadn't even started working for him, she corrected herself. But when she glanced back, he was waiting for her answer.

'I phoned my sister and she gave me news I didn't want to hear.'

He raised an eyebrow.

Lara rubbed her forehead. 'I was due to get married last week. Unfortunately, the night before the wedding, I found my fiancé in bed with my bridesmaid. It was all very awkward.'

'That sounds like typical Brit understatement,' Cal said. 'So you came up here?'

'Yes, I ran away,' Lara said sharply, daring him to judge her. 'I didn't face them; I didn't fight for Jason, the way my sister wants me to. I left.'

Cal shook his head. 'I'm sorry, that must've been hard.'

Lara's shoulders went down. It felt good to tell her story. The poison bottled up with her thoughts was being lanced by telling it. There was no disapproval in his expression. She went on.

'Jason and I were childhood sweethearts. We were inseparable. We were friends as well as loving each other, and we always knew we'd get married. We didn't need to plan it, we just . . . *knew*. Kate was my best friend from school, and she was the person I wanted to support me on my big day as my bridesmaid. I had no idea that they were attracted to each other.

'Jason was so sorry afterwards. He told me it meant nothing, that it was pre-wedding nerves. He says he doesn't love Kate, it's me he loves. But I don't know what to believe any more. So I ran away. I stuck a pin in a map, and swore I'd go wherever it landed. So here I am,' she finished.

Did she realise how forlorn she looked? Cal wanted to reach out to her and smooth the pain from her features. The pinched whiteness was back in her face, and her grey eyes were bleak. The absent Jason had a lot to answer for, Cal thought grimly. What a scoundrel.

He almost put his arm out to comfort her. She looked so alone. But he knew it would be a big mistake. He'd end up getting involved in her life. No, it was better to leave it. Lara had run away from her wedding and her fiancé. She'd made the decision to start again here. It was brave, and he reckoned she could do it. There was a determined streak in that slender body.

He'd seen it when they met in the courtyard. She was stronger than she looked.

'Everyone deserves a fresh start,' Cal said, but even as he said it, he knew it didn't apply to him.

'Thank you,' Lara said, unexpectedly.

'For what?'

'For listening to me. Malorie, my sister, doesn't listen. She knows what's right for me and when I talk, she lets me but she's already got her answer prepared. So it doesn't matter what I say.'

'That sounds a lot like my brother Garrett.' Cal smiled ruefully. 'He can't understand why I'm over here in what he thinks of as the back of beyond. He wants me to go home and get back to my life with him. I can't get through to him about what I need right now.'

What did Cal need? Lara wondered. He was a man who appeared to have it all: good looks, wealth, and a beautiful Highland estate — not to mention whatever he had back in America. But there was a solemnity to him, and then the fact that Helen was so protective of him, claiming he wasn't well. What had happened to make him travel so far from New York to the rugged moun- tains of Scotland? Was he running away too?

'What do you need?' she dared to ask, and held her breath when he didn't immediately answer.

His jaw tightened and she saw a muscle flex in it. He held himself otherwise still and she thought he wouldn't say anything. But then he stared straight at her with his clear blue gaze. The impact of it hit her midriff, but she didn't look away.

'That's a good question,' Cal said. 'I need what Invermalloch can give me.' He stood abruptly with a wince as his injured leg took his weight. He turned to look out of the window at the majestic sweep of boulders and heather and tough grasses. Then, with a visible effort, he turned back to Lara.

'I was engaged too, recently, to a

woman called Anthea. We'd only known each other a year, but she pressed and pressed me to get married. I thought I loved her, so I went along with it.' It would be impossible to describe how he imagined that Anthea filled the gap that his mother's lack of affection had created.

'Anthea liked nice clothes, jewellery and a high-maintenance lifestyle,' Cal went on. 'I was happy to give her that. We lived a fast life of work and play. It was all fine but then, recently, for some reason it wasn't enough for me. She called it cold feet, thought I was joking, that I'd change my mind when I called the engagement off.'

Cal remembered Anthea's bitter words only too readily. He'd accepted her temper, her slaps, because he felt guilty. But he wouldn't go back on his decision. He didn't want to marry her. He was barely aware of Lara now, listening silently, letting him talk. It was painfully good to spit the words out, to make himself say them.

'The day of the accident, I was in work, in our New York office. Anthea came to see me. She told me she forgave me for ending our engagement and that she understood how I felt. She wanted us to be friends and to go on seeing each other as part of our social group. I was relieved that she was finally being so mature about it. I hated that we'd fought, that there was so much bitterness between us.

'She brought a hamper of food, and suggested an impromptu lunch and a drive out of the city. Heck, I had enough work on to refuse, but I wanted to make amends somehow, to humour her and thank her for letting me go. So we drove for hours, up and out of the city, to find a place to picnic.

'I was driving and it was a slow, winding road fringed with white birches. Something made me glance over at her. Her face was contorted, and all of a sudden she was screaming that if she couldn't have me, then no-one else would either. She grabbed the steering wheel and as we struggled for control, the car went off the road and down a gully.

'I must've blacked out for a minute, but when I came round I was out of the car and my leg was useless. I looked back and saw Anthea was still in the passenger seat, but she wasn't moving. I started to pull myself along the ground to go get her out when the gas tank exploded.'

Lara's finger joints were sore where she'd laced them in a too-tight grip at Cal's account. It was horrific. No wonder he had left the States to hole up at his Highland home. But it was clear he couldn't escape his nightmares so easily. She understood now Helen's protectiveness of him. She obviously knew the whole story.

'I'm sorry, I shouldn't have told you all that.' He sounded surprised that he had.

Lara shook her head. 'Don't be sorry; I'm glad you felt able to talk about it. It's . . . horrible for you.'

It was Cal's turn to shake his head. 'I deserve to live with it. It was my fault. I broke the engagement, and I should've known how Anthea was feeling, I should've realised she wasn't dealing with it well. I blame myself for the accident, and for Anthea's death.'

'You're not to blame,' Lara argued hotly. 'It's terrible that she died, but Anthea was at fault, not you. Why punish yourself like this? Plenty of people end engagements or marriages every day. They don't all react the way she did.'

Lara was a case in point. She'd effectively ended her engagement to Jason by leaving Devon and telling no-one where she was going. Jason might be on her blacklist for having sex with her best friend, but she couldn't imagine him trying to murder her for leaving.

Cal's expression gave nothing away. He'd blocked her out. There was a sudden awkwardness between them now. They'd both exposed more than they wanted to. Lara had told more to Cal about her recent past than anyone else. From his stiff stance, it looked as if he'd done the same with her. Clearly, he regretted it.

He didn't speak but with a brief nod, left the cottage. She heard him murmur to the horse, and then the rattle of harness and the clip-clop of Kinash's hooves as they moved away along the path in the direction of the stables.

5

Lara stood nervously in the middle of her ranger's visitor centre, waiting for her first group. The centre was a converted tack room off the stables which had been emptied and brushed out for her use. The whitewashed walls were freshly cleaned and the floor-boards were clear of dirt. There were tables and plastic chairs set out, and a long trestle against the wall had trays, nets and identification charts laid out. There were five new pairs of binoculars waiting on Lara's desk, and a box of magnifying cubes for capturing insects for study.

She was dressed comfortably in blue jeans, trainers and a loose white cotton top, her hair tied back in a casual ponytail. Her fleece jumper was in her rucksack just in case the weather switched from sunshine to rain. In the

Highlands, it frequently changed several times a day, but she crossed her fingers it would stay nice for her first teaching session.

Cal had been more than generous in what had been provided. Helen had given her free rein to order whatever equipment she wanted, telling her that Cal had given the go-ahead. Malorie had sent up the stuff she'd asked for, and Lara was ready to get stuck in to her new job. She had seen Cal only at a distance over the last few days, and she guessed he was avoiding her.

She was sort of glad about that. She wasn't sure what she'd say to him when she saw him. Emotionally, they'd stripped themselves bare that day at the cottage, surprising themselves. There had to be a certain amount of embarrassment when they met again. He knew stuff about her that no-one else here did. She knew now what made him tick, and was pretty sure the other staff weren't aware of his whole story. The exception was Helen, of course, and possibly Bob Stanton. They seemed close to Cal.

The stable hands and the other workers liked him, though. When they talked about their employer, it was with respect and loyalty. In two months, he'd garnered their approval. The thing was, even though she was glad he was keeping his distance, she missed him. He spiced up her day when he was there.

Too much spice was bad for her, she reminded herself with a grin. Besides, she was sworn off men, and Cal didn't give the impression of wanting to get involved with anyone after the appalling experience he'd had with his ex.

There was a burst of laughter and chat from the courtyard. Lara tidied her hair quickly, and tried to look professional and welcoming. It was her first range ring group. She'd put up posters in the village, and Helen had driven her to the nearest big town to put up more in the tourist information centre there. There was no way of knowing whether there would be much interest in the guided wildlife walk she was offering as her first venture.

'Hi, I'm Lara,' she introduced herself to the interested group as they filed in and took their seats.

She counted ten people: it looked like two families and a couple. That was a good number. Not too many that they couldn't hear her speak or engage with them, and enough that it wasn't a waste of her time taking them out. She began to feel at ease. It was similar work to what she'd done in her last job in England, before she gave it up to marry Jason.

'Welcome to the Invermalloch Estate,' she went on, and they hushed to listen, 'I'm going to take you on a walk which will last about an hour. We'll take binoculars so we can look for birds, and we'll take pond nets and trays and see what we can find in the pools.'

One of the children put their hand up. 'Can I carry the nets?'

Lara laughed, 'I most definitely need

helpers, so all you kids can carry something for me.'

They rushed forward enthusiastically and she gave out nets, trays and the magnifier cubes. She distributed the binoculars to the adults and kept a pair for her own use.

'Right, please can you follow me. We're going to walk past the house and take a path which will lead us out onto the moors, where there's a scattering of pools for us to sample.'

She felt a rush of the old excitement as she led the way from the ranger centre across the courtyard to the lodge, with her chattering customers following behind her. Guided walks were fun because she never knew what kind of wildlife she'd find to show them. There was the thrill of discovery anew every session.

'I'd love to get in there and have a look around,' one of the women said to another as the group passed Invermalloch Lodge. 'There must be so much history to it.'

'Yes,' the other agreed, 'but look at the state of it. It's practically falling down. It needs renovation.'

'I heard it's owned by a rich American.' The first woman's voice held all the intrigue of the inveterate gossip.

'Well, it certainly doesn't look like he's spent any cash on it.'

Lara pretended not to hear the conversation, but she looked properly at the lodge as they went past. Her first impression of the eccentricity of its design hadn't changed. She knew too how odd and ancient the inside of it was. The visitor had a point. It was neglected and could do with repainting, retiling, and goodness knew what else. It would make an incredible place to open to the public if fixed up.

'Let's take the path now,' Lara said brightly, hoping to channel the women's interest back onto the safer topic of wildlife watching.

The path, of course, led right past her own cottage before it shimmied through heather to get to the pools. She could sense the group's interest in the little house, but didn't tell them it was where she lived. The gossipy woman nudged her friend as they went by, and Lara knew she thought it a crumbling property, too. Even the path needed upgrading.

They had to leave the trail to get to the actual ponds. Lara had a great idea, which she wanted to put to Cal. There were five pools close to each other, rich in pond life. It would be great to extend the path that led to the mountains by splitting a section of it off around the ponds. There could be a wooden dipping platform for educational use, and maybe a picnic bench or two.

She organised her group into pairs and gave them the nets to fish out whatever they could find in the water. She put water into the trays ready for the catch. Before long, they were all absorbed in finding water boatmen, diving beetles and dragonfly larvae in the water. Although the species were different to what could be found in the South of England, Lara was able to name them all with the help of identification charts.

'I'd love a seat,' one of the men said. He was quite overweight and sweating in the sun.

'I'm afraid it'll have to be on that stone there,' Lara told him apologetically. Watching him sit gingerly on the lumpy stone, she felt even more of a resolve to speak to Cal and try to get wooden benches there.

★　★　★

Back at her cottage at the end of the day, Lara washed her face tiredly. It had been fun. She had taken four groups for walks, and the third lot had seen a golden eagle. They shared her enthusiasm and eagerness to learn about Invermalloch's rich biodiversity. Now she was drained of energy and hungry.

After a quick meal of pasta and ratatouille, she showered and changed her clothes then brushed her hair and applied a light brush of face-powder and a touch of lipstick. There was no harm in looking good while she persuaded Cal of her plan.

Knowing she had a real reason to speak to him gave her the confidence to go up to the lodge to find him. Maybe she could forget that she'd told him all her vulnerabilities. But then, she couldn't forget what he'd been through. It made him more approachable. He'd gone through a painful experience and was still healing from it. Perhaps what she had to say would help take his mind off it. After all, Helen had been pleased when he took more interest in the running of the estate.

The door to the lodge was open, so she went into the hallway. She almost bumped into Helen, who appeared from her office with her light jacket on and her bag slung over her shoulder. A giant pair of sunglasses was balanced on her head. It was a beautiful evening and the sun was still high in the sky.

'Oh, Lara. Can I help you? I was just leaving for the day.'

'I was looking for Cal. Is he about?'

Helen smiled. 'He's upstairs working in his study. I'm sure he won't mind if you go up. Third door on the right. It'll do him good to have a break, he's been in there all day. Bob's been working with him, but he's gone home now.'

'He's learning about the running of the estate from Bob?' Lara asked.

Helen shrugged. 'Some, but I don't know if it'll make any difference. He'll be going back to New York in the autumn, I imagine. Now, you must excuse me, Lara; I've got dinner guests and I haven't shopped for the food yet.'

Lara's mood dipped as she climbed the stairs. Cal was going away in a matter of weeks. It shouldn't matter. She would be leaving, too; but the thought still niggled. The summer was so short.

She knocked softly on the study door and waited. Cal opened it and she saw a look of surprise when he saw her. But his blue eyes were warm as he invited her in.

The study was a man's lair. It was all dark oak furniture and wall-to-wall bookcases. There was a fireplace with logs yet to be lit, and portraits above the mantelpiece. Lara decided they were MacDonald ancestors, as they were brooding and dark-haired and handsome. A huge desk took centre place on the floor, covered with papers and a laptop.

'Am I disturbing you?' Lara asked. She hoped he'd say no. There was something very comfortable about this room that made her want to sink into one of the velvet cushioned chairs by the fireplace to talk to him. It was good to see him again.

'I've finished for the day,' Cal said. 'I need an excuse to close down my laptop, so I'm glad you came by.'

He pulled a chair over for her. Her arm brushed his as she took it, and a little shiver went through her. He was casually dressed in sport cotton trousers and an open-necked shirt that showed the hollow at the base of his neck — which did something strange to her insides. Hoping he hadn't noticed the flush that rose in her skin, Lara mumbled her thanks and sat. Yes, the velvet seat was as lovely as she'd thought. She could get used to living like this. Now, where had that notion come from? For a moment, she imagined being at Invermalloch for longer than a couple of months. With Cal. Which was ridiculous. She needed to snap out of the odd mood that had gripped her.

'What can I do for you?' he asked, pulling up another chair to sit opposite her. Their knees almost touched. He had long thighs and their muscular strength was obvious. Lara tried to concentrate on what she'd come to say, but then Cal was speaking again. 'Before you tell me what it is, I wanted to apologise.'

'What for?' Lara asked.

'For telling you about Anthea and my accident. It wasn't fair to load that onto you. You've got your own worries.'

'Are you sorry you told me, or sorry I listened?'

Cal gave an exasperated sigh and ran his fingers through hair that was so thick and dark, Lara imagined pushing her own hands through it. That made her insides liquid, and she moved restlessly in her seat. Perhaps she shouldn't have come up here tonight. Whenever she was close to him, the air between them had an almost electric zing. Was it just her, or did he feel it too? She should fight it. Remain professional. After all, she'd come to discuss work issues. *So stick to the point*, she told herself.

'That's sharp of you, Lara. You're right, I guess I'm sorry I let it all out of the bag. But you're a good listener. I . . . I haven't shared what happened with many people over here. Back home, it's like everyone knows. It was splashed all over the newspapers, such big news; I couldn't escape it. That's why Invermalloch is a haven for me. I get peace to work it all out.'

'And then you go home.' Why that should matter, Lara didn't know. But she'd miss him. There. She'd admitted it. She liked him, and that was okay, wasn't it? It didn't mean she was going to act on it.

'Yeah, I go home.' Cal nodded, but didn't look particularly happy. 'My father wants me home already, and Garrett is on my back, too. My businesses won't run themselves much longer remotely, so I do have to go back.'

'They'll miss you here,' Lara said lamely. *I'll miss you.*

'I'll miss them too,' Cal admitted. 'Helen and Bob do a wonderful job running the place. I'm just finding out how difficult it all is.' He indicated the papers on the desk. 'So, why did you want to speak to me?' he added, fixing her with a firm gaze.

'I had an idea I wanted to run by

you,' Lara said, the enthusiasm building as she visualised her plan. 'It's to do with the ponds near my cottage. I took a group there today to look for wildlife, and we had a great time — but there are no seats, no facilities. I was thinking you could put in a path around the pools, and maybe a picnic bench or two for people to rest at.'

There was a pause as she tried to gauge his reaction. But Cal gave nothing away, his gaze steady on hers. Lara continued, nervously: 'Then there was something one of the customers said that got me thinking about the lodge itself. About how if you did it up, you could open some of the rooms to visitors. You could lay them out historically so people could see how Invermalloch looked in the past. It could be a huge visitor attraction for the area.'

Cal's face was stony. Lara's heart sank.

'You don't like that idea, do you?'

'It's crazy,' he said bluntly. 'This is

my home; why would I open it up to strangers?'

'I thought it would generate income,' Lara tried to explain. 'I mean, look at it, the place is falling down from neglect.'

She thought she'd gone too far when his brows darkened and met, and his voice was cold as he answered: 'The MacDonalds have enough wealth to renovate Invermalloch if we choose to do so. But we don't choose.'

And it's none of your business. Lara could hear the unspoken end to his retort. He was right, it was none of her business — and yet Invermalloch had got under her skin somehow. She wanted the old place to thrive, and it was frustrating that she couldn't get that across to Cal.

'I thought you loved it here?' she cried, standing up, hands on her hips in challenge. There was a brief glimpse of amusement in his expression, but it was quickly masked. He didn't stand, but deliberately sat back as if relaxed. That irked her.

'I do love it here,' Cal said quietly. 'But I don't live here, and it's not a priority for our businesses.'

'What about all the boyhood summers you spent here? What about the memory of your grandparents? Don't they deserve better for the place they raised you?'

She'd gone too far. Cal stood up, his eyes flashing in sudden anger. She was aware of how tall he was, and the broad strength of his chest as he stood so close to her, but she didn't budge a step back. He had to listen to her. She knew instinctively she was safe with him. He wasn't the kind of man to be threatening, however large he was.

'You don't know my family, you didn't know my grandparents, so what gives you the right to tell me how to manage my affairs?' he said bitingly.

His nearness was having a powerful effect on her. It was as if the molecules in the air were vibrating wildly between them. The electrical zing at full blast. She didn't care if he was angry with her, she was annoyed with him too for not listening to her ideas.

With a muffled groan, Cal stepped forwards and pressed his mouth down on hers. Lara opened her lips in surprise but he took it as an invitation and his tongue sought hers urgently. His mobile lips moulded to hers, seeking and tasting hotly. Lara kissed him back with a passion that shook them both. He pulled her body to his and she felt the lean, hard strength of him. His kiss gentled and then he drew back. Lara missed him instantaneously. They stood and stared at each other.

6

He shouldn't have kissed her. It had been an impulse he couldn't control, but he regretted it.

Cal was eating a late dinner that his housekeeper had left for him, but he wasn't tasting any of it. He was remembering the softness of Lara's lips and her fierce response to him. She wanted him as much as he wanted her. But it had to stop.

He pushed his plate away, his appetite gone. What was it about her that got to him so? Even in faded jeans and a simple blouse, with her hair pulled up by an elastic band, she attracted him. He liked women who dressed up, made up their faces, and took care of their appearance, didn't he? He'd never gone for the natural look. There weren't many women in his social circle who didn't dress to the nines even for breakfast.

Lara was gone. She'd practically run from him after they kissed. He'd let her go and decided it would do them both good to have a breathing space. So he hadn't pursued her or tried to make it right. He was reminded of how he'd run from her that day at her cottage when they'd told too much to each other. They were almost strangers, had known each other a little more than a week, so why had he confided in her so readily?

Cal sighed. He had answers to none of it. He flipped open his laptop which he'd brought down to the kitchen with him. Might as well work. It would focus his mind on something other than a slim, English girl with big grey eyes and pale blonde hair. Besides, he was becoming more and more interested in the running of the estate. A part of him even dreamed of moving here permanently to live and manage it. But it was just that, a dream. The MacDonalds lived in New York and worked their businesses from there. He could quite imagine Donal's response if he said he was moving across the world to a wilderness in the north of Scotland.

★ ★ ★

Lara hadn't gone back to the cottage. She was too dazed by Cal's unexpected kisses. They had been both fire and sweetness. Her lips tingled with the memory of his mobile mouth pressed firmly to hers. She had *never* been kissed like that. In fact, she'd only ever kissed Jason. He was her first and last boyfriend, and they'd grown up together. But Jason's kissing was familiar — and, if she were honest, predictable. It didn't set her aflame. It didn't lift her soul until it broke free above her in dizzying heights.

Telling herself it was only a kiss hadn't helped. She walked the path to the foothills, reliving Cal's embrace, and remembering that she'd more than met him halfway in desire. For a woman who'd renounced men, she wasn't doing too well. But then again, she wasn't looking for a relationship with him, or a binding trust. Her body had simply reacted to his. There was a chemistry between them, that was all. It meant nothing unless she wanted it to. And she didn't.

She knew what she wanted. She wanted to work at Invermalloch and live in her rented cottage until the autumn. Then, when her contract was finished, she would make her decisions. By then, she'd have possibly forgiven Jason, and would go south. Or, more likely, she wouldn't; and then . . . well, she'd find somewhere new to start over. Either way, it didn't involve Cal MacDonald. He'd be long gone, back to New York and his glitzy life.

The sky had dimmed to violet and a first few twinkling stars appeared. The looming mountains were charcoal shapes of peaks and jagged ridges. Although it got dark late in the north, when night came it fell swiftly. Lara stopped reluctantly. She had no torch, so if she didn't want to be caught out by blackness and have to crawl home, then it was time to turn back.

She was footsore when she reached her cottage. She turned the key and went inside, flicking the switch in the front room. Nothing. Lara frowned and switched it again. The room remained in darkness. She tried the lights in the kitchen and bathroom, but the electricity was out. Blast! What was she to do? She lifted the telephone receiver in a vague hope it might still be connected, so she could call for assistance; although the idea that an electrician would be available at midnight in a remote Highland location was thin to say the least. It was a moot point. The telephone was out too.

Lara stood for a moment, undecided. She had no heat, either, as the cottage was equipped only with old-fashioned storage heaters. The temperature tended to drop sharply at night, and it was already cold in the room. She had no way of heating a kettle for drinks, and the cooker was electric too, so no hot food.

There was no other solution. She was going to have to go back to the lodge and ask Cal for help. Lara squirmed at the thought. She hadn't spoken to him when their kiss ended. She'd just run from him. What was she going to say now? Pretend it never happened? *Coward. You can handle this. You're a big girl.* She didn't feel it.

With a deep breath that filled her lungs nicely, Lara marched back along the path to the big house. In the gathering dusk, the turrets and carved ledges cast black shadows and the gargoyles leered like demons. It was so gothic, she almost laughed hysterically. Then she muttered a small oath as she realised the door was locked. Cal had gone to bed. What would he think when he was woken to find Lara wanting in?

Then she remembered Cal's housekeeper, Mrs McGaddie. It was more than likely that she lived in, so maybe she'd answer the door. She might not need to disturb the Laird in order to give Lara a bed for the night. Feeling better now she'd sorted that out, Lara rang the bell. She heard its sonorous tones inside, echoing down the long hallway and probably bouncing off the suits of armour.

It felt an age until she heard the housekeeper fumbling with the locks. The door opened. It wasn't the old woman. It was Cal.

Lara took another rush of breath. He had a bathrobe on — which wasn't fastened, so he was bare-chested — and his hair was rumpled. His feet were bare, too, which made him seem oddly vulnerable. He scratched his head at the sight of her and drew his brows together in puzzlement.

'I've no electricity, it's gone out.' The words rushed out like she couldn't get enough air.

'Happens sometimes. Didn't the generator go on?' Cal asked, yawning.

'Oh, I ... I don't know. I didn't

investigate thoroughly.' She felt foolish. Of course they'd have a back-up in a remote place like Invermalloch. Probably the electricity went out on a regular basis.

'Doesn't matter, come in. I'll get someone over in the morning to fix it for you.' Cal hesitated. 'There's plenty of bedrooms; in fact, you can use the one you slept in the first night you arrived.'

'Thanks.' Lara slipped past him as he stood unmoving in the doorway. He moved then to avoid contact with her. So, he felt awkward too. It didn't put her any more at ease.

'Did you bring overnight things?' he asked politely.

Lara felt foolish all over again. 'No, I just left. That was daft of me. I'll go back and get my toothbrush and nightie.'

He caught her arm as she made to turn. The contact singed them both, and he let his hand drop as if scalded, but her arm felt ring-marked to Lara.

The heat rose in her face, but it was shadowed in the hallway so he wouldn't notice.

'Lara . . . don't go. I mean, there are new toothbrushes that Mrs McGaddie keeps in the bathroom upstairs, and I can find you something to wear.' He swallowed and turned from her to lead into the lodge. 'She's not here tonight; her grandson's not well, so she's gone into town to help look after him.'

'Right.' Lara nodded brightly. She meant to convey that she could handle all this — Cal half-naked walking ahead of her; her probably borrowing his own clothes to sleep in; the fact that Mrs McGaddie was gone and they had the house to themselves. *It's all fine.* She gave a nervous little cough and felt a wild giggle rise up in her throat. She swallowed it down.

While she was thinking this, Cal stopped so suddenly she bumped into his back. She gave a muffled apology. He pulled open a cupboard and gave her a folded shirt.

'This will have to do. It's one of my shirts, so it'll be way too big for you.'

Lara nodded casually. 'It's fine, thanks.' As if every day of her life she wore the shirt of an attractive man to sleep in.

Cal hesitated, 'About earlier . . . '

He meant their kiss.

'It didn't mean anything, I know,' She rushed in over his reluctant words, 'It was a mistake and I'm happy to forget it happened, if you are?'

'Agreed.' His tone was clipped, but he didn't need to look quite so . . . *aggrieved*, Lara thought. After all, he'd kissed her, not the other way around. *Well, not at first*, she corrected herself, trying to be truthful.

'So, here's your bedroom. I hope you'll be comfortable,' he said politely.

Lara nodded, equally polite. She waited until he'd left before slipping out of her clothes and pulling on his brushed cotton shirt. It smelt of fresh laundry and was crisply ironed, pre-sumably by the housekeeper. Cal wore this shirt, his skin touched it where hers did . . . Telling herself to get over it, Lara leapt into the chilly bed and rolled the covers round her, hoping to generate quick warmth. She was highly conscious that Cal was only a couple of rooms away in the silent house. It was comforting and arousing in equal measure.

★　★　★

Cal lay in his own bed and stared up at the ceiling, unable to sleep. He was far too aware of Lara a short distance down the hall. Was it a mistake letting her sleep there? But then, he reasoned, he could hardly have refused to let her into the lodge. Either she slept there overnight, or he went and fixed the damned electricity there and then in the pitch darkness. Or, more likely, simply spiked the generator up and got it going. Why hadn't he thought of that?

Cal sighed. He had to admit, there was a part of him liked having Lara so close. The part of him that couldn't resist her. The part that had made him kiss her earlier. It galled him that she so readily dismissed it as a mistake. She wanted to forget it had happened, and he'd agreed to. But he couldn't forget. The kisses had turned him inside out, made him crave more. Though apparently they hadn't had the same effect on her, if she was to be believed.

He regretted the kiss, he reminded himself firmly. It was wrong for both of them. He was hurting over Anthea, and Lara had a lot of emotional baggage too, with her cheating fiancé. It wasn't right for either of them to get involved.

Having sorted this out to his satisfaction, Cal rolled over and fell asleep. But his dreams were furiously active, and soon one recurrent nightmare flashed up. It was the same every time. He was in the car again with Anthea. He smelt her perfume, cloyingly sweet in the enclosed space, and he turned to tell her it was over. Then the black smoke and the acrid stink of fire consuming metal and plastic. He cried out to Anthea, telling her to move, move before it was too late. As ever, the nightmare closed with him falling into space, knowing he was going to hit the ground moments later . . .

Lara had drifted into a light sleep when she heard the shouts. She sat up, disorientated in the unfamiliar room. The heavy drapes blocked any moonlight, and she could barely see her hand in front of her face. Then more shouting. It was Cal. She stumbled out of bed and along the cold corridor. Without thinking it through, she ran into his bedroom and went to his side. He was thrashing about, and she caught his arm with both hands to still it.

'It's okay, it's okay,' she said gently, holding him tightly until he relaxed in her grasp. He didn't open his eyes, and threw his head side to side on the damp pillow as if arguing with someone. He was fast asleep.

Lara stroked his hair and murmured comforting nothings to him. She knew what to do. Malorie had suffered nightmares as a child. The small modern bungalow where they had grown up had thin walls, and Lara had often rushed from her bedroom to Malorie's to calm her sister when the bad dreams struck.

Cal sighed deeply in his sleep and his body slackened. The nightmare was gone, she reckoned; yet she let her fingers lie a little longer on the softness of his hair. There was such a contrast between that soft texture and the hardness of his muscled arm where she'd stopped its agitation. A wave of tenderness for him washed through her. From what he'd told her, he'd been through hell with his ex-fiancée.

She was gradually conscious that she was in his bedroom, sitting on the edge of his bed while he was sleeping in it. Not only that, she was wearing only a shirt, *his* shirt. It hardly reached down as far as the top of her thighs. If he woke up . . . Lara stood, as quietly and gently as possible, and tiptoed out. With luck, he wouldn't even remember she'd been there.

* ★ ★

She was tired in the morning, as if her sleep had done no good at all. She had to dress in what she'd been wearing the previous day, and cursed that she hadn't thought to bring a change of clothes from the cottage. As she went down the stairs, she smelt coffee and the distinct aroma of frying eggs. Her stomach growled. Yes, she was hungry. Had Mrs McGaddie returned to her duties? But no — when she went to the enormous kitchen she saw Cal, dressed already in work trousers and blue shirt, with hair damp from his shower.

He had his back to her, working away at the huge old-fashioned range with a skillet of eggs, a loaf of bread sliced on a board beside him. He heard her and turned with a grin.

'How do you like your eggs? Over easy, or sunny side up?'

'Smells great. I just like them fried, thanks.'

Cal laughed. There was a lightness in it, an infectious quality that had Lara smiling too without knowing quite why. Except that he didn't laugh enough, so it was good to hear it.

'Come over here and I'll show you what I mean.' Cal indicated the skillet where four eggs bubbled in a small puddle of oil.

Lara went and stood beside him. Her head came up to his shoulder, and she had a childish impulse to stand on tiptoe and make herself taller. He flipped two of the eggs to seal the yolks.

'These guys are over easy,' he pointed to them, 'while these two with the yellows smiling are sunny side up like the sun, see?'

'I like it,' Lara exclaimed, grinning back up at him. 'Can I have one of each, please?'

'Sure can, as long as you fix us some coffee to go with them.'

Sunlight was pouring in through the

window. Outside, a flock of hens cackled to each other, and in the distance there was the noise of one of the estate Jeeps revving up for the day's work. It was idyllic, Lara thought happily as she took it upon herself to lay the table for two breakfasts. She liked being here. It was peaceful and beautiful and the best hiding place from her problems with Jason that she could possibly have found. It didn't hurt to share her morning with Cal, either. She sneaked a glance at him. His damp hair had curled a little, and she had a flashback to the previous night when she'd soothed him by stroking it.

He brought two plates to the table with eggs and buttered toast, and they ate.

'I'll get over to your cottage this morning and get the electricity fixed,' Cal told her.

She quelled a little bubble of disappointment. No excuse to stay another night at the lodge. Anyway, Cal's housekeeper would no doubt be back today. It was wrong to want to overnight again so near to him. But she couldn't help the little mood dip.

'I'll be busy with my guided walks, so I won't be there,' Lara said. 'Does that matter?'

'Unless you're an electrician, then no, I don't need you,' he teased.

He didn't need her. But he had last night. As if she'd spoken her mind aloud, Cal put his cutlery down on his cleared plate and gave a quiet cough.

'I think I owe you thanks? I had a nightmare last night, one of the worst I've had for ages. Were you . . . did I dream you were there beside me?'

Lara blushed tomato-red. She looked at her empty plate, unable to meet his eyes. He'd been fast asleep, hadn't he? If she'd known he had sensed her there, she'd have left fast.

'Lara?' His voice was soft.

She gazed up at him then, to see the softness reflected in his eyes.

'Malorie, my sister, used to get terrible nightmares when we were children,' Lara said. 'I was the only one who could soothe them away. You . . . you were suffering, so I didn't think, I just . . . hoped I could do the same for you.'

'And it worked a treat,' Cal replied.

His expression was unreadable. He looked away from her then, out of the window or maybe at the dancing sunbeams on the burnished sinks.

'I've got to go.' Lara stood up hastily. 'My first group is due in ten minutes. I need to set out the equipment.'

He didn't try to stop her. She clattered down the stone entrance steps and into the bright, lovely sunshine. Once inside her visitor centre and out of sight, she pressed her hand to her beating heart. Now she was in danger-ous territory. She could deal with her physical attraction to Cal MacDonald, Laird of Invermalloch. But now, she actually *liked* him.

7

'The identification keys aren't difficult once you know how to read them,' Lara said cheerfully, holding up one of the laminated cards to show her mid-morning group. There were only six people in this group, but she was glad of a quiet session. The previous group had had twenty, and that was too many for one person to handle. If the season continued with so much interest from tourists and visitors, she would have to ask Helen to consider taking on an assistant ranger.

'So, if the animal you've found has six legs, then it's an insect,' Lara went on, pointing to the relevant section on the card. 'But if it has eight, then it's going to be a spider.'

A hand went up. It was a girl of about six, with red hair tightly plaited and a liberal sprinkling of freckles across the bridge of her nose. 'Are we going to look for animals today?'

'Don't worry, we're going outside in a few minutes.' Lara smiled. Her younger audience never wanted to sit and listen, they always squirmed to grab nets and trays and get out to see the wildlife. She didn't blame them. That was the part she enjoyed most too.

She picked up a bug box, ready to to explain how to use the marked grid on the lid to measure the mini-beasts, when someone came into the centre and sat at the back. Lara looked up to greet the late arrival, and saw it was Cal. For a second, she didn't know what to think. Was he here to check up on her? But there was nothing but mild interest radiating from him. He seemed relaxed as he crossed one long leg over the other and put his head to one side, listening. Lara heard herself talking calmly about the bug box, and tried to zone back in.

'Okay, we're going to go for a walk over to some ponds now. We can dip for creatures or hunt in the grassland for insects. Everyone take a net or box, and follow me, please.' She tried to sound calm and confident, but Cal's presence had thrown her. She was pretty sure he wasn't there to cause trouble, but she was so totally conscious of him that it made it hard to concentrate on her lesson.

As she led the way to the pools, she was suddenly anxious. Despite Cal's insistence that he would do nothing to change Invermalloch, she had made a few small improvements in her own time. Several visitors had complained of the lack of seats once they reached the pools. Lara had found some old railway sleepers at the back of the courtyard and asked one of the stable hands to cut them in half. He had then volunteered to move them in the truck to where Lara wanted them placed.

The sleepers made perfect benches. Lara had stacked smaller blocks of the wood to make bench legs, and then the main sleeper was placed lengthways on top. There were four seats around the pools. An older woman, in charge of three lively children, sank gratefully onto a bench as soon as they got there.

'Gran, come and see this!' one of the boys shouted.

'Give me a minute, Sandy. I need a rest first. Thank goodness for the picnic area.' This last comment was directed at Lara, who nodded her agreement.

Behind her, Cal murmured in her ear, 'I had no idea I owned a picnic area. I'm glad I joined the group today. I knew I'd learn something.'

Lara turned quickly to him. 'I can easily dismantle the benches. But for the next few weeks, I'd like to leave them up for my customers. They really appreciate them.'

Cal was amused. Did she realise how fierce she looked when defending what she believed in? Her pale blonde hair was mussed by the light wind, and wisps of it framed her face. Her cheeks were pink from the walk, and her grey eyes shone with her passion as she spoke. She was so much smaller than him, he could lean his chin on top of her head. Or nestle her into him easily. She'd be a perfect fit. He felt a swift protectiveness towards her. It lasted only a minute because he shoved it away fast. The problem was, that morning, he'd felt a strange tenderness for her.

The nightmares about Anthea and the accident occurred frequently, and derailed him in their intensity. Usually he battled them out to wake sweating and with pulse running wild, utterly exhausted. But Lara had taken the terror out of his dreams simply by being there. He'd woken feeling refreshed, with no fast-beating heart to worry him. Even more weirdly, he'd felt happy. An unusual emotion for him these days. The tenderness that had enveloped him as he watched her eat her eggs was unexpected.

She was watching him curiously. Cal realised she was waiting for his answer about the benches. Her group were absorbed in catching insects or pond dipping. The wind soughed gently across them, bringing a sweet scent of myrtle with it. He wanted to kiss her. Her soft, full lips demanded it. He almost leaned down to do so. But the chatter and laughter of the group brought him to his senses.

'Cal? The benches?' Lara said, impatiently.

'Leave them up. You're right, people seem to like them.'

He almost laughed at her astonishment. He felt heady today. He watched Lara guide her group, teaching them patiently and sharing her enthusiasm for the natural world. She was a very likeable young woman, and people responded to that, Cal told himself, knowing he was being pompous. Why not admit it? He liked her too. He liked her compassion last night, he liked her courage and stubbornness, he liked her company.

Cal thought it through as he sat on one of Lara's home-made benches, watching the activity at the pools. He liked her. He found her attractive. Doing the math, the next step was to ask her out, to act upon it. But he wouldn't. His trust in other people had been severely damaged by Anthea's behaviour. Even if he could trust Lara, how would she react if they got closer but he didn't end up being in love with her? Would she turn crazy like his ex? There was no point in starting anything if he got more deeply entangled at every step, only for it all to end in disaster. Besides, he considered, they'd be going their separate ways in only a month's time. He was almost ready to go home. And Lara's contract was up at the end of the summer. He had the feeling she'd go south then. Back to her fiancé.

★　★　★

It had been an odd kind of day. Lara had returned to her cottage by early evening, and was now soaking in a long, hot bubble bath. The heat and perfume

125

of the water warmed her weary muscles, and she felt her energy returning. She'd been tired all day, not having had much sleep the night before due to Cal's nightmare. She tried not to dwell on the feel of his hair under her touch, or the emotions that had diffused into her as she tried to help him sleep. The oddness had begun then. Only to be compounded by his surprise visit to her rangering group.

She still didn't know why he'd turned up. At least he'd been okay with her makeshift seats around the pools. Instead of disapproving and ordering her to take them down, he'd appeared almost carefree. He was incredibly appealing when he was relaxed and happy. She'd enjoyed having him there. He was friendly to her customers, and she'd heard him talking about the estate to them. He was kind and funny with the children, and had helped them sift through their net-catches in the white trays.

If he had come to check up on her,

he hadn't mentioned it. She hoped he could see that she was doing a good job, and that the people who signed up for her wildlife walks really appreciated the beauty of Invermalloch.

Helen had dropped by the cottage earlier, just as Lara arrived back from her last walk. 'Hi, I'm glad I found you, do you mind if I come in for a moment?'

'Of course. Sorry, I'm a bit muddy, so I'll try not to drip on you,' Lara said, opening the cottage door to let Helen in ahead of her.

'Your job is going well.' Helen sat on the sofa, looking around the room in appreciation. 'There's no shortage of visitors wanting to come on guided walks and wildlife tours of the estate.'

'It certainly feels flat out,' Lara agreed, pulling her boots off and putting them on layers of newspaper to keep the mud off the floor. 'Is everything okay?' She felt a little nervous in case Helen was there to tell her otherwise. She couldn't bear to lose her job. She loved it.

'No, no, it's all good,' Helen said reassuringly. 'In fact, I'm here because the tourist office in the town wants to put up an activity schedule on their website for Invermalloch's countryside ranger service. They've had a huge level of interest in your posters.'

'Wow,' Lara said, pleased and amazed in equal measures. 'That's great.' Then she frowned.

'What is it?' Helen said. 'I thought you'd be enthused by that.'

'I am,' Lara said hurriedly, not wanting Helen to think she was being negative. 'It's just that I can only deal with so many people in a day. If demand increases, you may wish to take on another ranger.'

'We'll think about that.' Helen nodded and stood up, glancing at her watch. 'I've got to go. My kids play tennis today, and I need to pick them up.'

She paused on her way out. 'Did you see Cal today?'

'Yes, he came along to one of my walks this morning. Why?'

'I just wondered. He seems better recently. It's as if his healing has accelerated.'

There was a brief silence. Lara didn't know what to say. She hadn't been at Invermalloch when Cal first arrived. She had no idea what state he'd been in, but Helen had always implied he was in a bad way. How had she described him to Lara? *The laird who wasn't well*. No wonder Lara had envisioned an ancient soul wandering the estate before she actually met him.

'He's been through a lot. That Anthea was an evil woman, from all accounts. His father phones me every day to ask how Cal's doing. Don't tell him that, he'd hate to know he's being monitored. The point is . . . it would be terrible if something or someone set his recovery back. Do you know what I mean?'

Lara understood only too well. Helen, in her soft, lilting Highland accent, was warning her off, on behalf of the powerful MacDonald family in New York. She wondered if Helen had told Cal's father about her. But what was there to say? Nothing had happened between her and Cal. And nothing would. She wanted to get that across to Helen, but saying that made it sound as if she'd thought about him in that way.

'You look tired. I shouldn't keep you,' Helen said. 'I'll see myself out.'

Lara watched her from the window as she hurried away down the path, straight-backed and balancing perfectly on her heels. Cal certainly invoked a lot of loyalty and love in his staff. That was when the deep weariness hit her, and she ran her bath and almost fell into it.

★   ★   ★

Lara got dried on one of her new fluffy towels. That was the other nice part of having a job. She could afford to buy a few luxuries. It was good to be in control of her finances again. Jason had persuaded her to give up her previous ranger post. He joked she'd be a kept woman once they got married. She had felt a twinge of regret when she handed in her notice, but she'd had the cosy image of being Jason's wife, keeping a warm and welcoming home for him and hopefully for their babies.

She pulled on a pair of black jeans and a crimson woollen top. Her last walk of the day had taken her group away from the direction of the pools. For a change, she'd marched them steadily to the higher ground at the feet of the mountains. There were ptarmigan and red grouse to see, and a herd of deer, the stag with five-point antlers standing majestically on a ridge with the light behind him.

An older Canadian couple had given her a generous tip, and refused to accept it back when she tried to decline.

'Honey, we'll never forget that view of the monarch of the glen,' the wife told her warmly.

'It was worth every cent,' her husband agreed, pressing the notes into Lara's hand with a kindly wink.

Lara had been inspired by the sight of the mountains. She had a good stout pair of new hillwalking boots and a pair of looped wool socks. She also had a day off tomorrow. She was determined to go walking in the hills.

She was planning what she should take with her when there was a knock on the cottage door. She opened it to find Cal standing there, loose-limbed, his hair ruffled by the strengthening evening wind.

'Put your jacket on and come with me,' he ordered her.

'And a good evening to you,' Lara retorted with a little bite of sarcasm. He merely crinkled his eyes at her, and her breath caught at the mesmeric deep sea-blue of them.

She shrugged on her jacket, buttoned it and followed him out. He didn't wait to speak but moved on and up the path, clearly assuming she was following his vigorous steps. Lara tried to keep up, but the man had ridiculously long strides. She was half-running by the time they got to the pools. Then she stopped stock still.

The water bodies shimmered in the lowering light. The mauve heather shook in the gusts of wind, and a single curlew peeled a thin cry and flew off. But, magical though the surroundings were, Lara didn't see them. She was looking at the magic that Cal had wrought. Her makeshift benches were gone. In their places were four sturdy seats, with iron supports, arm-rests and varnished wooden planks to sit on. There were also two picnic tables with metal barbecue stands attached.

She couldn't help it. The tears welled up, and she rubbed them away as she turned to him.

'You're crying,' he said, scratching his head. 'I thought you'd like it.'

Lara gave a muffled laugh and wiped

away the last tears. 'I do like it. Thank you. It's the most lovely picnic spot I've ever seen. Why?'

'What do you mean, why?' He kicked at a pebble and it shot into the nearest pool, leaving ever-increasing circles on the water surface. He wasn't looking at her.

'I mean that you didn't seem too enamoured of my improvement plans for Invermalloch last time I broached the subject,' Lara said drily. 'So, why do this for me?'

'Who said it was for you? Maybe I saw a need today for the visitors, and solved it.'

'Okay.' Lara's happiness dipped. What did it matter why he'd done it? *Because I wanted him to have done it for me.* It was silly and illogical, but that was how she felt.

She threw him a glance from under her lids. He was grinning at her. Her stomach did its gymnastic thing.

She mock-punched his arm playfully. Cal rubbed it. 'That hurt.'

'No, it didn't. But you deserved it for teasing me.'

'Would I tease you? I wouldn't dare do that to Invermalloch's very determined countryside ranger.'

She pretended to punch him again, but he caught her hand. For a moment, their skin melded in heat, and he started to draw her to him. Lara held her breath. But Cal stopped. He let her go and turned briskly to the outdoor furniture.

'It's solid stuff, the best make my guys could get. It'll last many seasons.'

'Cal?' The question was like a catch in her throat. But her whisper was dissolved by the gathering wind, and he didn't hear her.

'It's getting cold, we should go back,' he shouted over the rasp of the air.

She should offer him coffee. It was the least she could do as a thank-you. Yet did she want him in the intimacy of her little house? *Grow up, Lara. It's the right gesture. Besides, he'll probably decline; Mrs McGaddie will no doubt have his late dinner ready up at the lodge for him*. So she was surprised when he accepted her offer immediately.

The wind hurtled around the stout stone walls of the cottage, rattling the windowpanes and making the roof creak. Lara was worried in case tiles came flying off.

'This cottage has stood a couple of centuries,' Cal assured her, interpreting her expression correctly. 'You may lose a few tiles, but we can fix that easily. The rest of the structure is solid.' He ducked to look out of the window, and grimaced. 'Looks like we're in for bad weather tomorrow.'

'Really? Are you sure? I saw a forecast in the newspaper, and it said there'd be sunshine and showers tomorrow. I was hoping to go hillwalking.' Lara clattered the pottery mugs and cafetiere down on the coffee table and sat down.

Cal shook his head. 'That's a low-level forecast for the village and surrounds. The hills get their own weather forecast. There can be a huge difference between the weather down here and that at the mountain peaks. I wouldn't risk it.'

Lara didn't reply, but she wasn't put off by what Cal said. If it was bright and sunny when she got up in the morning, she was going to go hillwalking. The hilltops weren't that far away, and she wasn't intending a long day's hike. She just wanted a good view from the summit.

'So you like the picnic area?' He changed the subject. He sounded so eager that Lara wanted to laugh. Not at him, but with him. She liked his new enthusiasm.

'I love it,' she said. 'And the customers will too. I can't wait to use the new area with my next groups. Pity I'm not working tomorrow: I'll have to wait a whole day to see their reactions.'

'You love your job.' Cal sounded intrigued.

'Yes, I do. I had to give up my last job

when I got engaged to Jason, and I regretted it the minute I handed in my resignation. I find wildlife fascinating, and I love sharing it with people and helping them discover the wonder of it all.'

'Why did you give it up when you got engaged? Surely you could've kept working?'

Lara sighed. 'Jason wanted us to have a traditional marriage. He was going to be the breadwinner, and I was going to stay at home and keep house. I liked the idea. I suppose I had this image in my mind of how cosy it was going to be.' She shook her head. 'Silly of me.'

'Not at all,' Cal said. 'It works for some couples. That's the thing, isn't it? Talking everything through and making decisions together.'

'Is that what you and Anthea did?' Lara dared to ask.

Cal took a swig of his coffee and put the mug down carefully before answering.

'I guess that was part of the problem

with me and Anthea. We never talked. Not properly, and not about anything that mattered. We enjoyed a good life together, don't get me wrong, but it was all about the money and the travel and the parties. And for a long while, that was enough. Then one day it wasn't. For me, at any rate. Something changed, I can't tell you why or when exactly, but it was . . . different. I realised how meaningless my life was.'

'Did you talk to Anthea about that? What did she say?'

Cal gave a short laugh. 'She didn't get it. Not only did she not understand what I was trying to say, she panicked. She could see all the good stuff she liked vanishing. She didn't want to take up good causes or modify our lifestyle. Soon she was going to parties and functions without me. We were drifting apart well before I realised I didn't love her. But she wouldn't give me up.'

The wind suddenly gusted against the cottage, making Lara jump. It broke the intensity of the moment, and Cal looked up.

'Hey, I'm boring you with my old history,' he said with a forced smile. 'What's that weather doing? I've got people coming for a deer hunt tomorrow, and we need a good calm day with not too much wind.'

'You're going to kill the deer?' Lara asked in dismay.

Cal shook his head at her. 'Invermalloch's a working estate, Lara. There are too many deer, and they have to be culled to keep the herd healthy. Guys pay to hunt them with the estate stalkers, and the venison is top quality.'

'I hate the thought of them being shot,' Lara said with a grimace.

'That's because you've a tender heart,' Cal replied softly.

Lara's chest warmed at the look he gave her. Why did he have so much power over her body's reactions? She could almost believe he was as attracted to her as she was to him. But when he talked about Anthea, she knew he'd been badly hurt by his ex, and guessed he was so stung he wasn't in the market for another relationship.

'Will you miss this place when you go home?' she asked, to distract herself as much as him.

Cal nodded. 'I sure will. It's all beginning to make sense, the way Bob's explaining how the estate is run. It's a smooth operation, but it needs an injection of some serious cash. You were right about the lodge, it needs to be renovated. But it's not just the house; the lands and the machinery could all do with upgrading and better maintenance.'

'So why don't you do it?'

He sighed. 'I can provide the funds for Bob, and I will do that when I get back. But there's a part of me would love to stay and run this old place myself.'

Lara perked up at that. 'Why don't you?'

At least Cal would be on the same continent and in the same country as her if he stayed. Maybe she'd be taken back on as ranger in future seasons, too. Her mind ran ahead, imagining how it could be.

His answer doused her in cold water. 'Because I've too many commitments back in the States. It's just a dream, nothing more.' He stood up. 'Thanks for the coffee. I'd better get back before Mrs McGaddie sends the dogs out to search for me.'

Lara stood too. They both hesitated, standing there so close, yet not touching. He turned away first, opening the door and letting a blast of icy air swirl in. She shivered and he headed outside with a brief nod of his head to her.

8

Lara woke the next morning to clear skies and bright sunshine. It was too good a day not to go hillwalking, and she had to make the most of her day off. Cal's warnings about the hill weather seemed mistaken as she glanced out the window at the distant summits, which were clear of cloud.

She made sure to have a good breakfast of cereal and toast to give her energy for her walk. Her new woollen socks slid on easily, but her leather boots were stiff and unyielding as she pushed her feet into them. Lara made a face. Never mind, they'd loosen up as she walked.

She packed a small rucksack with essentials. A raincoat just in case, although it looked like she wouldn't need it; a map with the hill routes on it; and a brand new plastic compass. Then she put in a packet of sandwiches, a chocolate bar and a carton of juice. Her intention was to climb the nearest hill and have lunch on the summit before heading back down.

She slung the rucksack on her back, pleased that it wasn't too heavy, and laced her boots. She was ready to go. She took a deep breath of the fresh, clean air as she stepped away from the cottage along the now-familiar path to the pools and beyond. She really loved this place. It was a pity she had to leave it. *And Cal.* The thought tugged at her and she shrugged it off. Firmly, she put one foot in front of the other and tried to concentrate on a good walking pace. Thinking of Cal wasn't going to help.

Now that she *had* thought of him, though, she couldn't help looking over towards the lodge and stables. Hadn't he said that there was a hunting party going out today? Yes, she could make out a group of figures near the buildings, and there were four Land Rovers parked nearby. She wasn't close enough to see if Cal was there, but presumably he was about. She hoped the hunt wasn't going in the same direction she was. She wanted peace and tranquillity to enjoy nature, not the sound of gunshots and the images of their dead prey.

Soon she was way past the pools with their picnic benches, which made her smile happily all over again. Cal's surprise gift to her. He couldn't have chosen anything better. Then there was nothing but the creak of leather from her new boots, the call of meadow pipits and the sound of her own breathing as she plodded on. She hit her rhythm and settled into it. Once or twice she glanced up at where her route was taking her. The path dwindled to a stony track once it steepened in gradient. Then it snaked through the grass as it headed for the hill summit, which looked very far away.

Lara dampened down her doubts. It was going to be lovely when she reached the top. She just had to visualise sitting at the summit cairn, eating her sandwiches and enjoying the panoramic view. Her heart rate quickened with the exercise and her chest was painfully raw as she began to climb. Her lungs sucked in the air needily. She wasn't fit, she acknowledged ruefully; just as well she was walking today. If she achieved this, she promised herself she'd do more. There were several peaks all clustered near to each other. She'd do them all while she worked at Invermalloch.

After an hour of solid walking, her muscles were warmed and her breathing easier. She stopped for a rest and looked back. She was impressed by how far she'd come. The lodge and its scattered buildings and cottages looked tiny, laid out on a quilt of greens and browns of fields and wild country. There were the teardrops where the pools were, and further on, a larger expanse of blue water where Invermalloch Loch lay. She hadn't visited it yet, but it looked inviting, with a trim of white sands to one end and a tiny wooded island in the middle.

She wondered where the hunt had gone, and what Cal was doing right now. Shading her eyes with one hand, she thought she could make out tiny figures on the slopes away to her right. It was a relief they weren't going to interfere with her walk. She hoped the deer had got away.

Lara started climbing again, placing her feet carefully on the loose pebbly base of the track. She didn't want to trip. She found her pace and went on. Above her the summit loomed, all bare rock and stony bluffs. The track wound round below the cliffs and took a diagonal path over grassy slopes onto a summit ridge. Despite the harsh look to it, there was a relatively easy route to the top.

She was exhausted as she pulled up the last steep part to the peak. Then she caught sight of the stone cairn. She'd done it! She'd reached the top of the mountain! Lara cheered out loud. Then she thought of Cal. It would've been nice to share her triumphant moment with someone. And Cal would've understood. He loved this land. There was no-one else who would *get* what she was feeling the way he did. Malorie would be shaking her head in puzzlement at why Lara was doing this. Jason wasn't interested in wildlife, and preferred being indoors to outside. Her parents would only worry in case she fell off the mountainside.

'Way to go, Lara,' she shouted and punched the air.

Then, feeling slightly silly, she unpacked her sandwiches and sat beside the cairn to eat them. The view was fantastic, and she munched contentedly while staring around.

It wasn't until she'd finished her chocolate bar and drunk her juice that she saw the fog drifting in. The temperature suddenly dropped. Lara pulled her coat from the rucksack and put it on. But she was still cold: it was only a rain jacket with a thin lining.

With alarm, she saw the fog close in around her. It was fast and dramatic. One minute, she had the most marvellous view on earth; the next, she could see nothing but cobweb-grey light.

Trying not to panic, she grabbed at the map and compass.

'I'm okay, I know where I am, I just have to orientate the map and find north with the compass.' Talking out loud might be daft, but it gave her a level of calmness that she desperately needed.

'Here we are, the needle swings to the north, so according to the map I need to aim *that* way.'

Conversationally, Lara pointed with the plastic compass in the direction she hoped she had to go. There was nothing to see but a blanket of mist. Wherever she trod, she was going to have to be careful not to fall or twist an ankle. *Damn*. Cal had been right all along. She should have taken note of the mountain weather forecast.

Rain hit her, hard and cold, making

her shriek with its intensity. Now the sky was black, the clouds scudding in, thickening the fog to soup. She stood up. It was time to move.

Her heels were painful. The new boots had rubbed them to blisters. The rain jacket felt slimy and cold against her skin, soaked as it was.

Lara felt a sharp jab of fear. It struck her that she was in trouble. Here she was at the mountain's peak in a steadily worsening storm. Her feet were bruised and pummelled. She didn't think she could walk too far on them. She was freezing and wet. Not only that, her map was now sodden too, and unreadable.

She started to walk away from the cairn in the direction she reckoned the downwards path was. A tall shape loomed dark out of the mist. She gasped, but it was only a jagged tooth of black rock. She didn't recognise it. Was she going the right way? The next moment, she was sure she was walking up the gradient and not down. She stopped, confused and panicky. She turned and went the other way. But that didn't look familiar, either.

She took out the map again. But the rain had destroyed the markings, and the paper was mush.

'I'm going to keep calm and keep walking down. As long as I go down, then I'll hit level ground and safety.' It sounded like good advice. And so much better when said out loud in a confident voice.

Lara stumbled along. She had to go slowly. Her boots were hardly visible in front of her. She went with her hands held out in front of her as if playing blind man's buff. What if she fell over a cliff? She thought of Malorie and her parents. She'd never see them again. What about Cal? There was a pang of loss there too. They were just getting to know each other, and now she might never see him again . . .

Lara gave a cry as she stumbled over on her ankle, wrenching it painfully. It throbbed like mad as she struggled on.

She saw something ahead and blinked. Her eyes were playing tricks, surely. There was a little cave on the hillside. Now she was at it, it was less than a cave: a small shelter carved out under the bottom of a massive grey boulder. Thankfully, she scrambled in on hands and knees, ducking under the natural stone ceiling.

She lay down inside. A smell of damp earth and moss rose up. What was this place? It was completely bare except for a tiny stone wall, merely pebbles and rocks stacked at the corners of the cave mouth. Someone had stuffed grass and mud between them to make a rough covering. But it was shelter. Lara sank down, exhausted, on the mossy floor. Outside, the rain pelted and torrents of water rushed off the slopes and down the valley.

* * *

Cal frowned up at the hills visible through his office window. The forecast had been correct. Early-morning sunshine had given way to hill fog and stormy weather, which was getting worse now it was late afternoon. He got up and leaned out from the doorway to call to Helen in her office: 'Helen, is the hunting party back yet?'

She came out to answer. 'They're on their way back. I got a call from Lenny, one of the stalkers, to say the paying guests have had a successful day and are very satisfied. They bagged two stags and three hinds. They'll be recommending Invermalloch in turn to their business partners and clients, which will be good for us.'

'That's good,' Cal replied, but he was thinking about Lara. Hadn't she mentioned going hillwalking today on her day off? He'd warned her not to — but had she listened to him?

'Have you seen Lara today?' he asked.

'She's not working, if that's what you mean. She's got a day off.'

'Yes, I know, but she mentioned she might climb one of the mountains. I hope I'm wrong.'

Helen looked worried. 'I did see her this morning. She was wearing boots and a rucksack, and walking along the path to the pools. That goes on and up the track to the hills, doesn't it? Surely she wouldn't go up the hills when the forecast was so bad?'

Cal looked grim. 'She didn't listen to the forecast. Or me,' he added under his breath.

'What should we do, Cal? Do you want me to call the mountain rescue unit?'

He shook his head. 'We don't know for certain if she has gone to the summit. She might have gone for a low-level walk. I'll get my gear and go look for her. I'll take my cell phone and call you when I find her.'

Helen frowned. 'What about your leg? It's a fair climb to the top of the nearest mountain.'

'It's good, Helen. It's strong again.'

Cal touched her shoulder reassuringly, and went quickly to get ready.

He hoped he was right about his leg. But he wasn't worried about it. He was worried about Lara. There were fatalities every year in the Scottish mountains. The weather could change in an instant and catch people out. Inexperienced walkers with the incorrect gear, usually. He didn't think Lara would have all that she needed for the harsh conditions up there.

He cursed out loud as he shoved thermals, spare clothes and rope, map and GPS, and other vital equipment into a large rucksack. If anything happened to her . . .

When he went back downstairs he found Helen and Mrs McGaddie with a bag of food and a flask of hot soup.

'Have you room for these? I'm thinking Lara will need hot food to give her energy.'

'Thanks, I'll just about fit these into my sack.' Cal took the bag gratefully and stored it away.

'And Cal . . . ' Helen said, as he slung the heavy rucksack on and moved fast to the door.

'Yes?'

'Take care.'

'I will, don't worry. Keep listening for my call.'

With a nod, he stepped out into the rain and whipping wind outside, and leaned into it. Now all he had to do was find Lara.

★　★　★

How many hours had she lain here? Lara tried to move into a more comfortable position and winced. Her ankle hurt badly. She reached down to touch it. The skin felt puffy and tight under her sock. It was definitely swollen, and she prayed it wasn't broken. Thankfully, it was dry under the rocky roof, but little stones dug into her no matter how she lay. The slice of sky visible from her position was a weird maroon colour as the storm continued to whip the wind and rain into a frenzy.

The discomfort of the grassy, lumpy ground reminded her of family camping trips as a child. The damp, smoky fires her father lit, frying sausages over a blackened pan. Later on, snuggling up with Malorie in their down sleeping bags, trying to avoid the bumps and hollows where they slept, and squabbling over who should sleep where to avoid the worst parts.

Lara began to shiver uncontrollably. Her cotton top was wet through, soaked by her rain jacket. Her trousers, too, were wet. If only she had a blanket or a towel. Perhaps the shivering would warm her up. If only the storm would die down. Then she could make her way off the mountain even if she had to hop all the way. But it would be madness to try right now. She'd be blown right off the hillside.

At least there was plenty of time to rest and think. Her thoughts took her back to Invermalloch. Had anyone missed her yet? She wished she'd told someone where she was going. She hadn't seen anyone that morning. How long before they noticed she wasn't there? With a painful jolt, Lara realised it could be the next day before the alarm was raised. When she didn't turn up for work.

What about Cal? Was there a chance he'd drop by her cottage to see her? Last night, she'd felt really close to him. He'd opened up to her a little, talking about Anthea. Then there had been that moment at the picnic area when she was sure he was going to kiss her. And she was going to let him. Heat went through her at the memory. Then she knew. She knew what her body had known forever. Cal was gorgeous, attractive, thoughtful, generous and oh-so-sexy. And she had fallen in love with him. Fallen in love so deeply she knew it was a forever kind of love. It was crazy. She had known him for only a few weeks, but it was enough.

★ ★ ★

Cal pushed against the squalls of wind. Where was Lara? He hoped to hell she'd found a place to shelter. If not . . . He refused to let his imagination go there. There were too many horrific possibilities. People got blown off hills or staggered into crevasses, or simply hit their heads on rocks. Nature was savage, especially in a remote place like this.

The rain lashed down against his face and Cal almost welcomed the harsh, cold, stinging sensation. It kept him alert. It was a far cry from the boardrooms of New York in his Savile Row suit, but he felt charged with adrenaline. He was fully alive. He and Garrett had climbed these hills in all weathers during their childhood summers. He was an experienced climber and knew the risks. As an adult he'd walked in the Appalachians at weekends, and loved the wilderness feel of them. Anthea had refused to go with him, and sulked mightily when he vanished on those breaks from the city without her. But he'd needed them. Even before he understood he had to change his life, the hills and the wild land had sustained him.

Now he had to find Lara. He wiped the rainwater from his eyes and stared about at the black-stained rocks. He blew out a breath. It was impossible. She was one small blink of life in a vast landscape. He guessed she didn't have a whistle to call for help. Six long sharp blasts was the accepted emergency call. What the hell did she think she was doing, coming up here without the right gear?

Cal swore loudly into the shrieking, billowing air. He started walking again, up a steep slope. His leg cried out, but held strong. The bones had knitted well. He was confident of his own strength.

He almost missed her. The wind had died down, but the rain was still hurtling from the purple skies in sheets. The hillside was one great rushing river of mud and dislodged pebbles creating a treacherous route. Cal was pushing upwards to the summit cairn when he glimpsed a dot of crimson under a ledge of black rock. He forced his way over to it, carefully avoiding a runnel of frothing, bubbling, peat-browned water.

There was a singing relief as he saw her blonde hair and her curled body under the red jacket. All at once, his body slackened. His muscles had been clenched tight in fear for her. She moved and cried out a little.

'Lara, are you okay?' Cal shouted into the shallow cave.

She turned her head towards him and he saw her large, grey eyes widen in her pale face.

'Cal, is it really you? You found me.'

'Are you injured?'

He scrambled under the stone roof, not waiting for her answer, and pulled his rucksack in after him. It blocked out the weather to some extent, but he had a better plan.

'I hurt my ankle,' Lara said, and he

heard her teeth rattling. She was shivering badly and he was worried by how white she was.

'Okay, I'm going to look at it, but first I need to get us some shelter.' He kept his voice firm and calm despite his concern. Working quickly, he unpacked his rucksack and took out the double bivouac bag. Using rocks and the metal frame, he managed to secure it over the exposed entrance to the cave. It cut the extent of cold air. Their body heat would soon help the temperature inside rise.

'Cal?' Lara's voice was shaky with cold, but she didn't sound scared. He felt a flicker of admiration for her courage, but it was mixed with annoyance at how she'd got into the predicament in the first place.

'You're angry with me, aren't you?'

'No.' Short and clipped.

He worked with the flask to get a hot drink for her. Hypothermia was a real possibility if he couldn't get her warm and quickly. Her shivering was the start of something more serious.

'Yes, you are. I can tell. You think I shouldn't have gone walking today.' Her voice was thready.

Cal's brows knitted. He had to keep her awake and conscious until she warmed up. 'You're a little fool,' he growled. 'What were you playing at, coming up here with nothing more than a thin coat and a knapsack?'

Her eyes flashed in shock, and Cal felt like a heel. She was cold and in pain and he was shouting at her. But at least she was now alert.

'I've got a compass and map. I made the summit, and I got myself here.' She sounded stronger, and angry.

Cal hid a smile as he screwed the lid back on the flask. That was better. He liked her when she stood up to him. She had guts. If she had the energy to argue with him, that boded well for her recovery. But when he turned back to give her the hot drink, Lara's head flopped forward.

'Lara!' Cal put the cup down fast and

reached for her. She was out cold. He didn't hesitate. She wasn't going to like what he did next, but it was essential to get her warm.

Cal unzipped her jacket and managed to peel it off her. Lara felt light and flimsy in his arms. The scent of her flowery shampoo wafted from her wet hair. He fought an impulse to kiss her head. She looked so sweet and vulnerable. Silently apologising, Cal stripped her to her bra and pants, got her boots off as gently as possible, careful of her injured ankle, and grabbed the sleeping bags from his pack. He interlocked them into one with their zips, and slid her into the soft, downy material. Then he took off his own outer clothing and got in beside her. His body heat would warm her and prevent serious hypothermia. Once that was sorted, he'd check on her ankle, but he was pretty sure from first inspection that it wasn't broken — just badly sprained.

He wrapped his arms around her

and hugged her close, willing his warmth to pass to her. Unfortunately, her closeness was having a real effect on him. Her body was silkily soft and the curves of her breasts pressed against his chest. She murmured into the crook of his neck, and with relief Cal saw she was coming round. There was a faint colour to her cheeks, and that was a good sign.

Lara was dreaming. It was a wonderful dream where she and Cal were dancing and he was holding her close, so close . . . She opened her eyes. She was momentarily disorientated. But, oh, so deliciously warm and cosy. Her mouth was against the strong dip of Cal's neck, and she sensed his muscles flex as she moved.

'Cal?' she whispered.

If only she could stay there forever. Folded into Cal's strong embrace, safe and protected from the elements. Little goosebumps rose on her arms as she became *totally* aware of him. Her legs were entwined with his. Her chest was touching his. His breath caressed her forehead.

'Lara, I'm sorry for this, but it was necessary.' It was said apologetically, but she noted he made no move to disentangle his limbs from hers.

'I know,' she murmured into his skin, wanting to burrow into the side of his neck, to trail kisses along the column of muscle there and down onto his chest. 'It's a cure for extreme cold exposure. I read about it in a survival book once.'

'You are warm?'

'Mmm. I'm not warm, I'm hot.'

That came out all wrong. Lara blushed, glad he couldn't see.

'Yeah, you sure are.'

She couldn't interpret that. Didn't want to. There was a shaft of disappointment when he made a space between them in the narrow cloth bag.

'How did you find me? I thought I was out of sight in the cave,' Lara asked, to distract herself from an overpowering need to cling to him, to smell and taste his skin.

'You were almost out of sight, except for the red of your coat,' Cal said. 'But this is a well-known howff, so I hoped you'd found it. If you weren't there, I was going to climb higher.'

'What's a howff?'

'Just this. It's a shelter under a large stone where you can camp overnight. It's a natural feature, but someone's added stones and turf to make it wind- and rainproof.'

'Cal?' Lara was drowsy. 'Would you have kept looking for me?'

He bent his head then and kissed her softly on her hair.

'I wasn't going to give up. Not ever.'

There was a silence, apart from the rustle of the sleeping bag and the eerie shriek of the dying wind outside. The storm was passing over but it was dark now. Lara looked up at him.

'We need to let Helen know we're safe.'

'It's done. I managed to get reception on my cell while you were sleeping. Just long enough to text Helen and get a reply before it crashed out. I said we'd be down at first light.'

'I hope I can walk on my ankle.'

'If not, I'll carry you. But let's get a look at it now you're warmed.'

9

The problem was that the sleeping bag was so . . . intimate. Lara's whole body was in contact with Cal's. Every fibre of her burned with this delicious fact. Probably, Lara told herself, the right thing to do was to get the dry set of clothes from Cal's rucksack on, and sit the night out under the howff roof. Away from temptation. But common sense told her it was warmer and safer here, right beside him. *Common sense? Or something more primal?* Suddenly it wasn't so safe. She moved restlessly and felt the strength of his muscles against her. Desire, strong and thick, rose up in her like a silken cord from her toes to the top of her head.

She turned her head at the same moment Cal dipped his to speak to her. His lips brushed hers and the spark in Lara ignited. Her lips parted. Did she kiss him first? Afterwards, she wasn't sure.

With a groan, Cal kissed her, his mouth firm and mobile on hers as he explored, taking and giving in equal measure. She felt the hardness of his body against hers. She wrapped her legs around his, her insides now flooded in liquid heat. She wanted him desperately. And there was no doubt he desired her too.

*   *   *

Lara curled right into the heat of Cal's chest. He put his arms around her protectively as a night owl screeched above the howff. She loved him. Her heart sang with it. Gradually, Cal's breathing slowed, and she knew he was asleep. But she felt fully awake. She was pretty sure he didn't love her. She didn't expect it. They had given in to a passion which had simmered between them since they met. That was all. If she harboured deeper feelings for him, then she'd hide them. She didn't dare hope he felt the same way about her.

And then there was the question of Jason. She hadn't thought of him once that day. Now that she loved Cal, she saw that what she and Jason had had was a different kind of love — she just hadn't wanted to admit it. She loved Jason as a brother. They'd grown up together. He was familiar, but he didn't make her heart sing. He didn't cause her skin to tingle at his touch. Poor Jason. He'd done her a favour by having an affair with her best friend Kate. Any lingering idea of going back down to England to try again with him was completely gone now.

Lara sighed, and Cal murmured in his sleep as his arms tightened round her. A shaft of intense love rocked her. She leaned into him and kissed him softly. She wasn't going to think about the future, about what would happen at the end of the summer. It was enough to be here with Cal, her Highland Laird.

Lara woke to a different day. The storm had vanished, leaving a landscape washed clean and bright. The sky was a vivid pale blue, shot through with thin lemon sunshine. The hills were live green and blotched with purple flowering heather. She snuggled back down into the sleeping bag. But Cal's warm body was missing. She scrunched open her eyes again. He appeared at the mouth of the howff, hunkered down and looked in at her.

'Hey, sleepyhead. You want coffee?'

'Coffee? Up here in the middle of nowhere?' How?' she stuttered.

A plastic mug of hot liquid was pushed into her fingers.

'By magic.' Cal nodded, indicating a small camping stove laid next to him on a flat stone.

He looked marvellous, Lara thought sleepily as she sat up to sip the drink. His dark hair was sticking up wildly and he had a growth of black stubble on his chin. He suited the padded checked jacket and faded blue trousers. *I've got it bad*. She smiled inwardly.

He crouched there, working the stove for a second boil of water. She grabbed at the fresh clothes he had brought for her, conscious that she was only wearing her underwear. As if that mattered, after their intimacy the night before. Still. She hurriedly got dressed under the cover of the sleeping bag. But Cal was studiously turned away from her.

She crawled awkwardly out of the shelter stone to join him. Her ankle was tender and puffy, but she could put some weight on it. Feeling shy all of a sudden, she sat beside Cal as the tin pot of water bubbled on the tiny stove. Was he going to mention what had happened between them? Should she? But telling him *I love you* was a bad idea. Lara had the feeling he'd run a mile if she confessed to that.

'How's your ankle?' Cal asked, frowning at it.

'Okay. I'll be able to walk down.'

Then he wasn't going to talk about last night. She tried to make it not matter. It hadn't meant anything to him. *So grow up, Lara.*

'I'll start packing up, shall I?' she said brightly.

'Lara?'

'Yes?' She paused.

Cal shook his head. 'Nothing. Put your wet gear in last, is all.'

She nodded, her hair covering those big, expressive grey eyes until she flicked it behind her ears with an exasperated gesture. He could barely meet her glance. She looked sad and questioning, but Cal wasn't sure he had the answer. What had he done? Last night they'd shared pleasure in each other. He didn't regret that unless Lara did. It was hard to tell. She was putting on a show of bright energy, but her eyes told a different story. What did she expect from him? He wasn't sure, only certain of what he couldn't give. Trust, love, commitment. He shook his head, angry at himself, and turned off the stove.

'You ready to move out?' His voice came out too harshly.

Lara flinched but gave a tentative smile. 'Yes, I think so. Do you want to check your rucksack? I'm not sure I've buckled it correctly.'

Cal grunted. He wasn't behaving well, but somehow couldn't stop himself. It wasn't fair to blame Lara. But, damn, it was all getting so complicated. He'd flown to Scotland to recuperate, to heal from both his leg injury and the events surrounding Anthea's death. His plan had been to stay a few months until the media furore died down and then fly home to the States, ready to resume work. End of story. Getting involved with a diminutive English blonde wasn't on the cards.

He wasn't *involved*, he reminded himself. But it was going to be damned awkward now, being around Lara. There could be no repeat of last night.

However, he wasn't brutal enough to voice this out loud. He had to simply stay away from her. There was enough work on the estate to keep him busy. She had her job to do, too.

'Let's go,' he said abruptly, avoiding Lara's unhappy stare.

She gave a little cry and stumbled as she slung her backpack on. Cal immediately righted her. He took his hands back fast.

'Can you walk?'

'Yes, yes, of course.'

But she was biting down on her bottom lip. He couldn't help but remember the taste and feel of her mouth under his.

'Give me your gear, I'll carry it for you and you lean on me.'

She looked like that was the last thing she wanted to do. Cal knew he was being snappy, but — heck! How else was he to get any distance from the urge to clamp his mouth firmly onto hers? To stroke her luscious curves and make love to her once more? It was torture enough, having her lean on him. She smelt of fresh air and myrtle and something flowery. Her head barely came up to his shoulder. It brought that protectiveness to the fore. Anthea had been a tall woman, nearly on eye-level with him. He'd never wanted to protect her. Always known she could do that capably herself. Despite Lara's size, she wouldn't like to know he had an instinct to look after her. She was stubborn, a fighter. Even now, clearly in pain with her ankle, she didn't complain. She was walking slowly, sure, but there was no moaning about it. She went steadily down the hill, with Cal adjusting his long stride to hers.

★   ★   ★

Lara was getting tired. The events of the previous day were catching up with her. Add to that, Cal's strange mood and she was thoroughly fed up. She trod down too hard and pain flared in her ankle. She stopped abruptly, and Cal had to stop too.

'I need a rest,' she said firmly.

Without waiting for his answer, she sat on the nearest large stone and rested her chin on her hands, her legs drawn up to her chest. That was better.

He sat near her, without speaking. When she slid a glance at him out of the corner of her eye, he was staring out over the view of Invermalloch splayed out below them. Not so tiny now. They had covered a lot of ground already in their descent, which was a relief. Lara didn't have much extra energy. But there was no way she was giving up. She'd get down to her cottage under her own steam. Though she had to know what Cal was thinking. About last night. They had to clear the air. Otherwise, how could they go on seeing each other every day?

'Cal,' she started.

'I know,' he interrupted, giving a shake of his head and running his fingers agitatedly through his already wild hair. 'I'm sorry I've been distant, after what we shared last night.' His blue eyes sought hers.

'About last night,' Lara said slowly. 'Do you regret it?'

Cal looked unhappy. 'Lara, I can't promise you anything. I'm strung out. After Anthea . . . well, I don't think I could ever let someone in that close again. I'm sorry. Can you understand?'

Lara nodded, even as her chest tightened in the cold.

'Yes, I do understand,' she replied quietly. 'Anthea broke your heart.'

A flock of birds pealed in song above them. It was a joyous sound, jarring with Lara's low emotions.

'I'm not asking you for anything,' she went on carefully. 'What happened last night was . . . chemistry. But we can be friends, can't we?'

The words were like sharp stones in her mouth. *Friends*. She loved him! But if friendship was all Cal could offer her, then she'd take it rather than be left with nothing.

'Friends.' Cal gazed at her hard.

Lara tried to keep her face serene. *Please don't let him see my inner turmoil; my need for him.*

'Yes, I'd like to be friends,' Cal said finally. 'But there can be no repeat of last night. It wouldn't be fair on either of us. Agreed?'

Lara forced a smile. 'You're right. We gave in to it once, but I'm not looking for a summer affair. Maybe we got it out of our systems,' she added, trying to joke.

No, she didn't want an affair with Cal MacDonald. She wanted all of him, body and soul. If she couldn't have that, then she'd settle for friendship. It would have to be enough.

'If only it were that easy,' he replied cryptically.

Before she could ask him what he meant, Cal had shouldered the rucksacks and was offering her his arm. Like an old woman, she clawed herself upright, her muscles aching and stiffened from their halt. Now she longed to get to the cottage and run a hot bubble bath to sink into for hours.

'Lara?' Cal paused.

'Yes?'

'Thank you,' he said simply.

Lara knew what he meant. *Thank you for not being like Anthea.* For not clinging to him emotionally, or forcing him to care for her. That wasn't Lara's style in any case. She was too fiercely independent for that. The one time she'd compromised that personal freedom, giving up her career to marry Jason, had shown her she was right to value her independence.

'We're nearly there,' Cal coaxed her as she faltered in exhaustion. 'See, there's the white of the cottage walls.'

He was right. It didn't take too much longer for them to find the familiar path to the pools and beyond to Lara's little home.

Her legs buckled suddenly as a strong cramp seized up the muscles. Lara slumped against Cal, and he grinned and lifted her up.

'Don't argue,' he told her, mock-severely, when she protested. 'I'm going to carry you the last hundred yards to your living room.'

'This is ridiculous,' she murmured, but let herself be carried, gently bumping against his chest with his every step.

'Hey, what are friends for?' he teased, a little emphasis on *friends* as if to remind her of their agreement.

'Not many of my friends pick me up against their manly chests,' Lara joked.

'That's because you're such a weight.'

'I am not,' she said indignantly, then caught the twinkle of amusement in his eyes.

'I think you've done my back in,' Cal groaned as they reached the cottage door. He put her down and staggered.

'Cal?' Lara said warningly. 'You are joking, right?'

He threw off the rucksacks and straightened up. 'Yeah, I am.'

'Oh, you rotter!' Lara grabbed a tuft of grass and threw it at him.

He dodged, and at the same instant, the door opened and the grass found a target. A fair-haired man, short and slightly overweight, stood in Lara's front doorway. Lara stared, aghast.

'Jason. What on earth are you doing here?'

10

'I came to visit you. Isn't it obvious?'

Jason sounded peevish. He glared at Cal. Lara had forgotten the wounded indignation Jason could weave around himself so easily.

'Did Malorie suggest you come?' Lara asked swiftly.

He flushed, and Lara knew it was true.

'I'd have come anyway. Look, Lara, you can't keep avoiding me. I'm your fiancé, for goodness' sake.'

'Ex-fiancé,' Lara reminded him.

'Who's that?' Jason ignored her comment and stared beyond her.

'This is Cal,' Lara said, turning to introduce him.

But Cal had gone. There was only her small rucksack, damp and forlorn on the ground. The tall shape of Cal's back was visible as he walked into the distance, back to Invermalloch Lodge.

'Is this where you've been hiding these past weeks?' Jason went back into the cottage, calling over his shoulder to her. For a moment, Lara stood there. The cottage no longer felt like a haven. Jason was inside it. She had an urge to run to the lodge, to Cal. It was fleeting and impossible. Jason was here, whether she wanted him to be or not. She had to face him sometime. It looked like that time was now. Wearily, Lara followed him inside. She was desperate for that hot, scented bath she'd promised herself.

Jason sat expectantly on her sofa. He patted the space beside him.

'Why don't you put the kettle on, and then come and let me see you. I've missed you.' His voice lowered to a tender, gravelly tone that used to make her shiver. Now it did nothing. Did he really imagine they could slip into their old ways again so easily?

'Who let you into my cottage?' Lara asked.

He raised his eyebrows at the sharpness of her voice.

'Helen somebody. Up at the big house. I told her I was your fiancé and she thought you'd enjoy the surprise. Said something about you needing it after your ordeal.' He stared at her anew. 'What ordeal was she talking about?'

Lara's weariness increased tenfold. 'Never mind, Jason. It doesn't matter. What does matter is that you can't stay here. There's only one bedroom.'

He looked hopeful, then puffed out a breath at her expression.

'Oh, very well. I can sleep on the couch, can't I?'

'Did you seriously think you could just waltz back into my life as if nothing had happened?' Lara asked incredulously, her anger rising. 'Did you actually imagine we were going to share a bed tonight?'

A wave of revulsion pulsed through her, shocking her. Until a few weeks ago, she had been going to marry this man. She had thought she loved him. Now, the thought of any intimacy with him was out of the question. She wanted intimacy with only one man. A certain Highland Laird who promised her only friendship.

'Kate was a mistake, a terrible error of judgement.' Jason stood up and came towards her, speaking softly, wiling her to forgive him.

Lara took a step back, shaking her head. She couldn't hear this right now. She was cold and tired and emotionally wrung out. She held her palms out to stop him.

'Look, Jason. I can't . . . I need to have a bath and get freshened up. Then we'll talk. I promise. Just give me . . . space.'

He nodded, seemingly satisfied. 'Okay. I'll just sit here, then, while you get sorted.'

She left him reading a magazine and gratefully locked herself in the tiny bathroom. The steam rose as the hot tap filled the bath, and she poured half a bottle of rose-scented bubble bath into the foamy water. She lowered herself into the water gingerly, and tried to block out all her thoughts for a blessed while.

She ended up nearly falling asleep in the bubbles. Eventually she wrapped a towel around herself and reluctantly drained the bathwater. She listened at the bathroom door but there was no sound. She tiptoed out and into her bedroom, dressing in a warm blue jersey with jeans tucked into her leather knee-length boots. She needed to speak to Helen, as she was meant to be working today. Lara hoped Helen had cancelled the guided walks: she couldn't summon up any enthusiasm to face groups of people today.

'Ready?' Jason appeared in the hallway.

The cottage was too small for two. Especially when one person didn't want the other there in the first place.

'You had a phone call,' he said, 'from the lodge. Inviting us both to lunch.'

He sounded pleased, as if they'd been invited as a couple. Who had phoned? she wondered. Helen or Cal? She had a dreadful thought. Perhaps they *had* been invited as a couple. Helen didn't know the full story. And Cal . . . did he believe Lara could so readily be persuaded into forgiving Jason's betrayal?

'We are going, aren't we? I'd love to get a look inside that old place.' Once upon a time, his puppy-like eagerness had amused her, and made her love him all the more. Now it irritated her. Jason wasn't getting it. He'd cheated on her with her best friend, the night before he was to marry her. Now he was here, acting as if they were on holiday together.

'Jason, we need to talk.'

'What, now? Shouldn't we go to lunch first? Talk after?'

'How can you stand there so casually when you had an affair with Kate?' Lara shouted, startling herself with a burst of hot anger. Shouting felt good. Very good.

'It was hardly an affair,' Jason blustered. 'It was one silly mistake, that's all.'

'A *silly mistake*! That's what you call having sex with my bridesmaid while I'm out shopping for our honeymoon? If I hadn't come home early . . . ' Lara shook her head, unable to finish her sentence. She felt rage building, but her voice had calmed remarkably.

'I was scared. Getting married's a huge commitment. Kate arrived to leave the bouquets and she comforted me. It just went a bit too far. That's not an affair, is it? I'm sorry you had to burst in on us. But it was nothing. It's you I love, Lara. It's only ever been you.'

Lara had a moment of utter and perfect clarity as she stood watching and listening to him. He was a weak man. He wasn't malicious or deliberately deceiving. He was weak. She had wasted ten years of her life on someone who didn't deserve it. Oh, she still loved him, despite his flaws — but it was in the same way she loved her sister. There was no sexual attraction left. Kate had done her a favour. Lara's eyes were now wide open to his faults, and to her own emotions.

'Well, are you going to say something?' he asked testily. 'I've told you I'm in love with you. I've apologised about Kate. Can't you forgive me?'

'I do forgive you,' Lara told him, and it was true.

She forgave him because it didn't matter any more. Her rage had vanished like ink into water. He put his arms out as if to embrace her, but she slipped past him and went to the door. There, she turned.

'I forgive you. But I don't want you back. We can still be friends.'

'Friends,' Jason echoed. He was stumped for a brief moment, then he shrugged. 'It's a start. I know I can win you round, if you give me time. Shall we go to lunch?'

★ ★ ★

Helen met them at the entrance to the lodge.

'I'm so glad you're safe.' She hugged Lara. 'I knew Cal would find you, but I was worried all night about you both, away up there in the storm.'

Lara caught Jason's frown as he realised she and Cal had spent the night together on the hill.

'But you're fine?' Helen asked, holding her at arms' length to check on her.

'I'm fine,' Lara assured her, touched by the concern. 'My ankle's a bit sore, but apart from that, I'm really okay — thanks to Cal.'

'I'm here to look after you now,' Jason butted in loudly. 'I can stay as long as you need me to. I've taken two weeks' leave from work.'

'Lucky you.' Helen smiled at Lara. 'What a nice surprise to find your fiancé waiting for you this morning. I didn't know you were engaged.' Her gaze flickered to Lara's left hand, which was bare of rings.

'We've been engaged for five years,' Jason said, and put his arm possessively around Lara. She fought the urge to throw it off. Whilst he didn't deserve such a public humiliation in front of Helen, she'd still tell her privately later how things actually stood.

'Before I forget, I cancelled your groups today,' Helen said, and Lara was grateful for the change of subject. 'I thought you'd appreciate a rest. I hope that was right?'

'Thanks, Helen, you're a star,' Lara said. 'But I'll make up for it tomorrow and pack in extra groups.'

Helen gave her an approving nod. Beyond her, Cal appeared. He'd changed into clean trousers and a crisp white shirt which accentuated his lean, dark features. Lara followed Helen inside, managing to lose Jason's grip subtly, but not before she saw Cal note it. Jason was oblivious, marking her step for step, and looking about at the eclectic furnishings.

The dining table was set for four. Cal

sat at the head of it, and Lara was reminded of that first meal she'd shared with him, Helen and Bob. He'd been a brooding figure then, and she had the impression that he'd reverted to that. Gone was her teasing companion on the way down the hill, and gone was the tender but passionate lover from last night. Cal was politely welcoming to her and Jason, as if they were guests barely known but to be given appropriate Highland hospitality.

Mrs McGaddie came in and placed plates of quiche, salad and hot rolls in front of them. Lara was all of a sudden starving. She'd had a cup of coffee on the hillside for breakfast, and hadn't eaten since. Cal was the perfect host, making sure they all had enough to eat and pouring drinks. Lara could quite imagine him at social events in New York, suave and sophisticated and confident. Not a scene she'd be comfortable with, that was certain. Not that it mattered. When was she ever going to go to parties in the Big Apple?

'So, you've known each other all your lives?' Cal asked conversationally, directing his question to Jason.

Jason nodded, happily spearing a slice of chicken from the warm salad. 'That's right; we grew up together, always knew we'd end up together. We've been engaged for a long while, too long.' He turned to Lara, fixed her with his gaze. 'It's my fault. I should've settled on a date and made her Mrs Wilmot long ago.'

'Jason,' Lara said, a warning in her voice.

But he went on blithely, as if she'd never told him she didn't want him back. Ever.

'We've had our ups and downs, but it's made us stronger, hasn't it, darling? We had a hiccup with our wedding, but I'm ready to organise it again; do it properly, you know.'

Lara could hardly swallow her food for what she was hearing. She put her cutlery down before she stabbed him with it. This was not the occasion for a heated argument. Maybe that was why Jason had chosen it to say what he felt. She couldn't blame him for persisting. But she didn't have to like it.

Cal's expression gave nothing away. Even when Jason's hand closed over hers and squeezed. Lara's stomach clenched and her appetite faded. Did Cal think she agreed with Jason? Did he care? He didn't want her. He'd made that plain. There could be nothing but friendship between them.

'When would you have the wedding?' Helen asked nicely. Lara could see that she warmed to Jason. Most people did. He was friendly and charming, and basically a nice guy.

'Whenever Lara chooses,' Jason said. 'What do you fancy, darling? Autumn or winter?'

Lara looked at Cal. His face was closed. He concentrated on buttering a roll, then pulled it apart and let it lie on his plate.

'Can we talk about this later?' she asked quietly.

'Of course.' Jason sounded triumphant, and she wondered if he honestly thought he'd won her over. Didn't he understand she wanted to avoid an embarrassing scene? Luckily, Helen began to tell him some of the history of Invermalloch when a porcelain vase caught his attention, which gave Lara a breathing space.

Cal couldn't eat. The buttered roll sat untouched on the plate. He should be happy for Lara. Her erstwhile fiancé had arrived and wanted to set things right, to marry her. If she had any sense, she'd forgive him, and head back down south to England to a cosy marriage and a man who could commit to her. Why that should give Cal a sense of loss, he didn't know. They'd taken pleasure in each other, sure. But he'd made it quite clear what he couldn't give. And Lara had accepted that. So why did he feel so rotten? Like he'd kicked her in the teeth.

In her arms last night, for the first night since the accident, he'd had no nightmares. Nestling his face into her soft, sweet hair had calmed him. The touch of her skin on his had kept him sane. But it didn't matter. It didn't change anything. He was still damaged by Anthea. The only thing he could offer Lara was a short, sweet affair. But she didn't want that and he didn't blame her. She deserved better. She should go home with Jason. Back to her English life.

'This is a welcome late breakfast,' Lara said to him as the other two continued their conversation and Helen showed Jason the family crest on the sideboard china.

'You mean the coffee didn't fill you up?' he answered.

They shared a smile, remembering the early-morning rise and the tiny camping stove billowing out steam.

'What's that? What happened at breakfast?' Jason asked, zoning in onto what they were saying as Helen excused herself to bring in more drinks.

'We didn't get any breakfast,' Lara

explained. 'We were up on the mountain where I got stuck last night because of a storm. Cal rescued me.'

Jason tucked in his chin and frowned. 'I'm sure it wasn't as dramatic as you make out. You looked perfectly fine when I saw you this morning.'

Cal looked at him. What did Lara see in him? He didn't deserve her. Cal sensed the other man's weakness, saw his receding chin and slight belly. He'd cheated on Lara. How could he?

'You should be proud of her. She was brave, and didn't give up under difficult circumstances,' he said sternly.

Jason flushed. He glanced back and forth between Lara and Cal and then sniffed. He didn't say much more until they had finished lunch and were headed back out of the lodge to the cottage.

Lara followed behind his stiffly-held back. He was annoyed, she knew the signs. But it didn't bother her any more. She no longer wanted to rush to comfort him. No longer felt the rush of guilt in case it was her that had caused his bad humour. Instead, she felt a heady freedom that he was no longer her problem. If he was lucky, Kate might take him on.

She pushed open the door with a sinking feeling. It was too small a space.

She turned to Jason.

'I'm going to ask Helen if she can organise a room for you up at the lodge. You won't be comfortable on the sofa. It's too short.'

'You mean you don't want me here,' he replied nastily. 'It's obvious from your behaviour. I've wasted my holiday leave coming up here ready to take you home. I apologised, damn it. What more do you want?'

Lara shook her head. 'I don't want anything from you. I'm sorry, but seeing you here, it's made me realise what I should've known a long time ago. I don't love you as a fiancée should. I'll always be fond of you but I can't marry you.'

'It's him, isn't it?' Jason spat. 'I saw

the way he looked at you. You accuse me of cheating on you with Kate, but I'm not the only one, am I? Can you stand there and deny it? You've slept with him. I know you too well, Lara. I know everything about you. I can read your face, you can't hide it.'

'I didn't cheat on you, Jason. We were already over and I was free to do what I wanted.'

'But you did sleep with him?' he persisted.

Lara nodded.

'Do you love him?' Now he couldn't hide a note of petulant hurt in the question.

'Yes, I'm in love with him.' She whispered it, not wanting to hurt him more.

'He's in love with you too,' Jason said flatly.

'No, you're wrong there. He doesn't love me,' Lara told him. It was painful to admit. The magic they'd shared on the mountain wasn't to be repeated.

Jason moved away from her and into

the living room. He began to pick up his belongings which were spread out over the furniture. He shoved them into his suitcase.

'What are you doing?'

'I'm leaving. I'm not staying where I'm not wanted,' he said huffily.

He looked at her as if hoping she'd tell him he was wrong. But Lara said nothing. She felt intensely sad that it had all come to this. She and Jason had a long history together. Yet it had frayed like cotton thread into nothing.

'Where will you go? Do you want me to ask Helen to book you a room in the village?' Lara asked numbly.

'There's an evening train back down south. I can catch that. I think I'd rather sit for three hours on the platform in this godforsaken country than stay here with you.'

Lara let his bitterness wash over her. Deep down inside, he must know that he was to blame for all this.

'Would you like a lift to the station? I

can get one of the stable hands to take you.'

He shook his head. 'Goodbye Lara. I hope you know what you're doing.'

★   ★   ★

After Jason had left, she tidied up the cottage, washed her working clothes and organised her notes for the next day's guided walks. Throughout it all, she didn't think of anything much. She focused on the simple tasks. In the early evening she took a long, gentle walk through the estate grounds, keeping deliberately away from the path to the foothills. She'd had enough hillwalking to last her a while.

It had turned into a mild summer's evening after the cold day. There was a raw beauty to Invermalloch while never failed to lift her spirits. Jason had called it a godforsaken country. He hated the countryside, was much happier in cities and towns where he could shop and spend.

She saw then that they would never have been good together. Eventually their different passions and interests would have divided them. He had never understood her love of wildlife. She, in turn, didn't much like cities.

How strange that Jason thought Cal loved her. He was usually a good judge of character and quick to notice nuances in people's moods. But he was wrong this time. Cal MacDonald didn't love her.

She circled round the back of the stables, pausing to stroke Kinash's soft muzzle. Then she went home. She stopped at the single rowan tree at the edge of the outhouses. The blossom was falling, and already a single berry hung from the branch above her. It was an early indicator. Autumn wasn't far off, and change was on its way.

11

The days passed quickly by. Lara was kept busy with groups wanting to see the estate and the wildlife, or to hear stories of its past, or learn how to stalk snipe and track eagles using binoculars. It was exhilarating and satisfying work and she immersed herself in it, losing all the sadness of her failed engagement in the sheer graft of the working day. She hadn't heard from Jason again and didn't expect to. But Malorie had phoned a few days after he went back down south.

'He's very upset, you know.'

Lara bit her lip on a hasty retort. 'I'm upset too, Malorie, but it would never have worked.'

'How do you know that? You didn't give him a chance to make it up to you. Honestly, Lara, you've thrown away the one man who loved you wholeheartedly. You're crazy.'

'I don't feel crazy. I feel relieved. I'm sure Jason will get over it, and when he does, he'll agree with me that we were right to call it off. I'm glad I discovered my true feelings before I got married.'

There was a shocked silence at the other end of the phone as Malorie gathered her ammunition. Then:

'I'm coming up to visit you. You're probably more upset than you think. Delayed reaction.'

'What about Tom?' That might put Malorie off from marching up and taking over organising Lara's life.

'I'll leave him with Mum and Dad. Not a problem. I can't come immediately as the other two staff are both off on leave, but once they're back, I'll ask the boss for a week off. I'll let you know when to expect me.'

She rang off quickly after that before Lara could protest. She guessed Malorie's plan. It would be a war of attrition, lots of comments about Jason's good points until she wore Lara down to a promise to go back to him. Well, that was never going to happen, and Malorie was going to have wasted both her breath and her holiday entitlement.

Still, Lara was secretly glad her sister was going to be visiting. There was a hollowness inside she couldn't shift. Cal was avoiding her. It was obvious. She hadn't seen much of him in the weeks following Jason's visit. When their paths did cross, he was pleasant but not forthcoming. He clearly regretted their night together and was trying to put distance between them. Very successfully.

So she was amazed when there was a knock on her front door on her recent day off and she answered it to find Cal there.

'Is there a problem?' she asked quickly, running through her list of work. Had she forgotten to lock up the visitor centre? Had she allowed the last group to leave litter at the picnic area?

'I deserved that,' Cal said with a grimace. 'I've been keeping away from you. No there's no problem. I . . . I wanted to see you.'

'Oh.' That statement, and the look on his face, lit her up inside. The hollowness began to dissolve.

'Are you busy? Can you join me for a boat ride?' he asked with an enthusiastic grin.

'I'm doing my laundry, so no, not busy. And yes to the boat ride,' she said, her heart running merrily inside her ribcage at his nearness. She should be angry with him for avoiding her, but she couldn't bring herself to be. The fact was, she was delighted to see him, whatever the excuse.

She grabbed her raincoat and joined him on the path. He was driving a small, mud-splattered off-road Jeep, and indicated for her to get in. They drove over the rutted path and along a forestry track in a direction she hadn't taken before.

'Where are we going? Isn't the sea in the opposite direction?' she asked, confused.

'We're not going to the sea. The boat's on Loch Malloch.' He pointed ahead to where the dense stands of pines thinned out, and Lara saw a glint of blue water. It was the loch they'd looked down on from the mountain-side.

Cal halted the Jeep in a small turning circle and leapt out. Lara jumped down.

She hesitated. 'Why now? Why today?'

'Because I've missed you,' Cal said. 'I've been trying to stay away from you. I thought I'd give you time to work things out with Jason, if you wanted to.' He shrugged. 'But you're still here, working for me. So, I reckon I can enjoy your company while you are here. If you'd like to, that is.'

'I would like to,' Lara smiled, glancing up at him. 'You may as well know that I'm finished with Jason. I'm not going back to Devon or to him.'

Cal looked away, then back at her. His blue gaze was clear and more intense than the waters of the nearby loch. 'Okay.'

'Yes, it is okay,' she said. 'I'm looking forward to spending the morning with you as friends.'

There, she'd said it. Laid it out so there could be no misunderstandings. Cal nodded carefully and pushed his dark hair back.

'Come on, help me lift the gear. We're goin' fishin',' he drawled.

'I've never fished before,' Lara said doubtfully.

'It's easy, I'll show you. You do eat fish, don't you?'

'Yes, but usually they're wrapped in clingfilm and packaging when I get them.'

'You're not going queasy on me, are you?' He playfully pretended to feel her forehead for a fever, but his touch stung her and they both drew back.

Being friends was one thing. But there was a line that neither ought to cross. As they clambered into the boat and pushed off, Cal made a mental note to keep his hands to himself. The feel of her seared into him. He hoped it hadn't been a mistake inviting her out today. The fact was he couldn't keep away any longer. He'd done what he thought was right. Given her and that loser Jason space to work things out. But no longer. She'd had weeks. She was still here. That told him all he needed to know. Jason had lost out. And serve him right.

There was an aura of sadness to her that he vowed to lift today. A couple of hours fishing on his new boat would do the trick. Then he had a surprise for her. He couldn't wait to show her. The fishing was a way of filling in the hours until the surprise was ready. He hoped she liked it as much as he did. In the meantime, he needed to keep a little space, otherwise the heat that simmered there might kindle — and neither of them wanted that.

Lara fumbled with the metal hook and lead weights, trying to tie them onto the nylon line the way Cal had demonstrated.

'Here, let me do that for you.' He

reached over and took the bait from her.

She watched as his expert fingers tied the metal to the line.

'Did you and your brother fish here as children?'

The boat rocked a little as Cal reached for the bait pail, and Lara grabbed the side in slight panic. The waters lapped and calmed, but she released her grip slowly.

'Going out on a boat was one thing I could never persuade Garrett to do,' Cal said. 'He has a real fear of water and can't swim.'

'So you went out alone?'

'Yeah, my grandparents had a small dinghy that I could handle as a kid. I loved playing about on this loch. I brought Anthea over to Scotland once on vacation, but there was no way she was messing about on the water or going fishing.' Cal glanced across to her. 'You're the first person I've had accompany me on a fishing trip here.'

'I'm glad you asked me to come along.'

Their gazes locked. Then Lara deliberately took up her fishing rod and began to turn the reel. It didn't mean anything that Cal had asked her along today. Plenty of people liked to fish. She looked out over the shining loch to the far shore. It was fringed with delicate rowan trees whose leaves had turned to golden yellow, scattering a few on the ground beneath them like a carpet. There was a stone jetty, with crumbling boulders near the trees.

'Autumn is most definitely here,' Lara said quietly, more to herself than to Cal.

'You've two weeks' contract left, is that right?'

'Yes. The numbers of visitors is tailing off already. There's no point in the estate having a ranger soon.'

'You're talking yourself out of a job. I could extend your contract,' Cal offered.

She was tempted. She could stay here at Invermalloch for a few extra weeks, seeing him and spending time with him. But it had to end eventually. She was only putting off the inevitable.

'There wouldn't be much for me to do if I did stay beyond the next fortnight,' she said honestly. 'You'll be going home soon too, won't you?'

She held her breath for his answer.

He was slow to give it, and her hopes rose. What if he wasn't going? Could she stay too? She knew what Malorie would say. That she was wasting her time on a man who couldn't give her anything.

'I want to show you something.' Cal pulled the ripcord on the outboard motor and the vessel glided through the glassy water in the direction of the old jetty. He brought the boat round and tied it up to an iron bollard.

'Come on.' He held out his hand for Lara to get out.

She paused. 'What about the fishing?'

Cal tossed his head impatiently.

'We'll come back after. Just come and see this.'

Curious, she let him lead her back through the woodlands. When they came out of the firebreak, they were at the back of the lodge. There were several vans parked there, with workmen walking in and out of the back entrance to the house. A man with a long stepladder went by and Lara saw, in the back of an open van, rows of paint cans. A pile of scaffolding lay on the grass.

She turned questioningly to Cal. He grinned in delight at her amazement.

'You're renovating the lodge?' she said. 'I thought you said the Mac-Donalds chose not to do that. That it wasn't a priority for your businesses.'

She was throwing his angry words back at him. Cal winced.

'Ouch. I deserved that. But I've been thinking a lot about this old place and what you said. You were right. It needs a healthy injection of cash to keep it going. So I've arranged for the house

215

to get a facelift.'

Impulsively, she ran and hugged him. His arms closed round her quickly, returning the pressure, and for a brief moment they let themselves be close. Then Lara stepped back. She had no right to enjoy his embrace so much.

'This is great. What a pity you won't be living here to enjoy it.'

She walked away around the side of the house, and Cal watched her go. He still wasn't sure about his decision. It was going to upset a lot of people, and yet his instinct was to follow it through. He went round to the front door to find Lara. There was no room to get in the back with all the throng of workers.

Helen was there talking to Lara. She waved to him.

'Isn't this exciting? I can hardly get any work done for peeking out to see the decorating going on.'

'You're not ditching the suits of armour, are you?' Lara asked. Of all the weird furnishings, she liked those best.

'Oh, no. The armour's getting cleaned

and will be returned,' Helen told her. 'But the hunting trophies are another matter.'

'We need to keep the best ones,' Cal reminded her. 'But some of them are rather moth-eaten so they can be thrown away.'

Helen and Lara exchanged relieved looks.

Cal grinned. 'Yeah, I can see you two are in cahoots over this. Will I get a say in the final design of my own lodge?'

The two women shook their heads in unison. 'It needs a woman's touch,' Helen said firmly. 'Don't you agree, Lara?'

'Absolutely. There can be no dusty old tartan, horrid dead animals' heads or bagpipes anywhere.'

'I rather like the eerie wailing of the bagpipes. Did I tell you I can play the chanter?' Cal broke in.

'What's a chanter?' Lara asked, bemused.

'Please don't ask,' Helen said, stifling

a laugh. 'Seriously, he's still practising.'

'I have been told my playing sounds like a strangled cat, but I'm not giving up,' Cal said.

They walked inside to the wide hallway. It looked even bigger now it was bare of artefacts. The wallpaper was in the process of being stripped off the walls, and some of it hung in damp strips. At the far end of the hallway, a man was kneeling to unpin the ancient carpet.

'Are you going to open up some rooms to the public?' Lara asked.

'That's a good idea,' Helen said, turning to Cal. 'It would bring in revenue for the estate. Invermalloch could start paying its own way instead of being the white elephant of Mac-Donald Enterprises. What did you have in mind?' she asked Lara.

Lara felt uncomfortable under Cal's scrutiny. After all, she'd raised this suggestion before, and he'd been unhappy with it. Her mind flashed to how that original conversation had ended. With Cal kissing her passionately. She longed for the touch of his lips again. It was a self-inflicted agony being so close to him, yet not allowed to touch him or make love with him.

She was, all of a sudden, glad she was leaving. There was no way she'd accept a prolonged contract. Being friends wasn't going to work. She was aware that Helen was waiting for an answer, and with difficulty pulled her mind back to the present.

'I was thinking along the lines of a visitor attraction. Visitors could get a tour of the estate, perhaps, and see the working countryside in action. Then they could see some of the rooms laid out as they looked in previous eras, and learn about the history of the Highlands and the part the lodge had to play in it. You could even offer coffees and teas and home baking in the front room there.' She warmed to her theme, becoming more and more enthusiastic as she described her plan.

Cal watched her animated face and

thought her quite stunningly attractive. He'd offered her friendship, but it was clear there was no way they could be 'friends' without sexual attraction getting in the way. He'd lied to himself, too. Thought he was being honourable and taking the moral high ground in avoiding Lara. Telling himself she needed space to decide about Jason. The truth of it was that he didn't trust himself around her. Didn't trust that he could keep his hands from touching her. Why had he offered to extend her contract? He was torn between wanting to be around her and needing to be far away from her, for both their sakes.

'I'd better get back to my bookkeeping,' Helen was saying reluctantly. 'They won't keep themselves. Cal, I think we should consider Lara's ideas. The books might balance better in the long term.'

'It would need some prior investment,' he said.

Helen nodded in agreement. 'Yes, but you're pouring cash into the estate

annually anyway. This way, the investment should pay itself off in a matter of
a few years — if we get the marketing
right and charge visitors a reasonable
entrance fee.'

'I don't know if I want strangers
barging about in my home.'

'They wouldn't be,' Lara said. 'You
would choose which rooms were open
to the public, and your private rooms
would be cordoned off — or locked,
even. You might only chose to open two
or three rooms in total. It would be
entirely up to you.'

'I'm beginning to think you're wasted
as a countryside ranger,' Cal said drily.
'You should be in tourism and marketing.'

'Sorry,' Lara said, 'I'm overstepping
the mark. It's just . . . '

'Hey.' Cal reached out to her. 'I'm
joking, I want to hear what you've got
to say.'

Helen gave her a wink which Cal
couldn't see, and went off to her office.
Lara had an ally. It was sad she

wouldn't see the plan come to fruition. She'd be long gone by then. It struck her that Cal would be, too.

'Why are you doing all this? You're not going to be here to enjoy it,' she asked.

'I've been doing a lot of thinking,' he said. 'I love this place. For so long, I've been pleasing everyone else — my father, Garrett, Anthea . . . Maybe it's time I did what I want to do.'

'And that is?' Lara held her breath.

'To stay here at Invermalloch. Run the estate the way Bob Stanton's shown me. I know I can do it with Bob and Helen's help. Your ideas took a while to simmer in my head, but they're good for business. I'm going to go for it.'

'But what about your businesses in New York? I thought you said you couldn't run them from here?'

'That's true. I'm intending to hand over my part of the Enterprises to Garrett. It's time he grew up and started to work hard. He's had it too easy, and I know my father agrees that he needs to learn the ropes now.'

There was mingled pain and pleasure in Lara at Cal's words. Wasn't this what she'd fantasised about? That he would stay in Scotland and that she could see him? She could easily get another ranger post next year, and in the off-season there was bound to be waitressing or hotel work to be found. But the hard fact was, there was no hope for her and Cal. He hadn't lied to her. He couldn't give her the love she wanted from him. And she already knew that friendship wasn't enough.

A telephone rang somewhere to the back of the hallway, loud and shrill. The sound stopped abruptly and Helen leaned out of her office with a handset. She looked to Cal.

'It's Garrett. Your father's been taken ill, Cal. I'm so sorry, but it's bad news. I'll book you onto a flight home today.'

12

Cal looked out of the tenth-storey window of the New York skyscraper at the snowflakes falling over the city. Down below, the streets were decked in holiday lights, the colours brightly cheerful in the darkness. It was a cheerfulness that Cal didn't share. He'd been back in New York for two months now, and it felt like all he'd done was firefighting — at his business, and for his father's health.

'Cal, you ready to go?' Garrett poked his head round the office door.

Cal pocketed his car keys and his cell phone. 'I'll drive.'

It was a short journey to the hospital where Donal MacDonald had a private room and round-the-clock nursing care. He was propped up on several pillows when his two sons arrived. There were tubes and drips and digital monitors, but the nurses had attempted to make the place more attractive by putting in vases of flowers and some of Donal's personal belongings, such as his own wingback chair for visitors.

'How's he doing today?' Cal asked the duty nurse at the desk on their arrival.

'He's made a little progress since yesterday,' she told him, 'Every day he's getting a bit better.'

But his progress was slow. He'd had a stroke, and although the doctors promised a near-full recovery, they warned that this would take months of recuperation and patient care. Cal had flown over from Invermalloch knowing that he wouldn't be back any time soon. His place was at his father's side and keeping the businesses running until Donal was back at the helm.

'How are you, Dad?' Cal took the hardback chair next to his father's bed while Garrett lounged in the wingback.

Donal managed to lift his left hand in greeting.

'That's an improvement.' Garrett leaned forward. 'He couldn't do that last visit.'

'That's great, but rest now, don't tire yourself out,' Cal said to the older man. 'Garrett and I will do the talking, tell you what we've been achieving.'

With Donal, life was never just about being and doing. It had to be achievements every day, constant improvement and profit. Cal thought it was no wonder his father had succumbed to a stroke when he lived his life at such a rate of energy and stress. The pity was, he'd brought his two boys up to live like that, too. Couldn't understand when Cal spoke about the Scottish estate and the peacefulness of it. Couldn't understand Garrett's lack of commitment to the MacDonald work ethic.

At least Garrett had taken over some of Cal's responsibilities. There was no way Cal could handle all the business needs alone. Some good had come from Donal's misfortune. But he'd paid a high price to get his younger son trammelled into working every day, taking charge of employees and budgets.

'The renovations are complete at Invermalloch Estate. Helen's sent over images of the lodge and it looks real good,' Cal said, talking and assuming that Donal understood what he was saying. The medical staff had assured him that Donal did hear what they said, and could understand fine but was unable to communicate back. 'Next summer, I'll take you over there and show you what I've done to the place.'

His father's face was immobile. Did he really hear Cal? Garrett started telling Donal about the weekly profits then, and Cal was free to drift into his own thoughts. Helen had more or less shut the lodge up over the winter, with the intention of reopening in spring for visitors. The publicity on various tourism websites promised a grand opening event in March.

But where was Lara? He'd asked

Helen last week if she'd heard from her. But, other than reiterating that she'd gone down south with her sister, Helen knew nothing. Lara hadn't left a forwarding address, only a mobile phone number because Helen had promised to have her back as ranger in the Spring. Cal had to be content with that.

He had phoned her shortly after returning to America when Donal fell ill. He missed her. Missed being with her, hearing her laughter and her enthusiasm for the estate. She loved the place as much as he did.

'How's your father?' Lara's first words were full of concern. She sounded far away over the transatlantic line. Cal swallowed hard.

'He's not good. He's had a stroke and he can't move at all.'

'Oh Cal, I'm so sorry for you. It must be so difficult coping with that. Is Garrett helping?'

'Garrett has surprised me with his support,' Cal said. 'In a crisis, turns out he's got strength I can rely on.'

There was a long silence. Cal wanted to say many things to Lara but he couldn't. What would he say?

'When are you leaving?' *Will I see you again?*

'I leave next week,' she said. 'I wanted to say thank you, for giving me the opportunity to work here. It's been wonderful.'

'You deserved the job. You did great and brought in lots of customers. Hopefully those same people will come back to the visitor attraction next year. Where will you go now?' He hardly breathed, waiting for her answer. He had to be able to keep in touch with her.

'I don't know. My sister is coming up to see me. Perhaps I'll go back with her. I haven't made any plans as yet.'

She sounded somewhat forlorn. But he didn't have the right to ask her to stay.

'I've got to go,' he said. 'Visiting hours at the hospital.'

'Yes, of course. I'll speak to you soon.'

She'd rung off before he could say any more. That was the last time he spoke to her. When he next telephoned Helen to catch up, Lara was gone.

Here was the catch: he had no right to ask anything of her. What had they really had? A few weeks of getting to know each other. So why did he have a hollowness that he couldn't shift? Damn it! He missed her.

Garrett drove them back to the office. Cal went up and sat at his enormous oak desk with his feet planted on the thick pile carpet. Outside his door, he could hear his personal secretary speaking on the phone, organising the next day's appointments. He stood up, unable to concentrate. Visiting Donal did that to him. He worried about the older man's health and what the future would bring. He doubted if Donal would ever be fit to run their Enterprises again. But most of all, seeing his father in that hospital room brought home to him, like nothing else, the swiftness and fragility of a life. It could all end tomorrow, for any of them.

Cal pressed the intercom connecting him to his secretary.

'Penny, hold any calls and cancel my afternoon meetings, please.'

He didn't wait for her to argue. He slung on his jacket and took the car keys. There was someone he had to see.

* * *

It was a beautiful, grand, old wooden-walled house with wide sills and latticed glass windows. It stood in acres of its own land that cried out *old money*. Cal drove up the long and winding driveway with its bare-limbed winter trees reaching for the leaden sky.

A woman dressed in a white fur coat came down the long stone stairway as he got out of the car. She was in her fifties with blonde hair carefully coiled high, drop diamond earrings, and a face sculpted under the surgeon's knife.

'Hello, Marguerite. How are you?'

'Cal. I've been waiting for you for a very long time.'

'I know. I'm sorry, I couldn't bring myself to face you before.' Cal reached out and embraced Anthea's mother.

'Do you want to see her?'

He nodded. Marguerite took him along the side of the house to the rear grounds where there was a walled garden, the entrance barred by a tall iron gate. She pushed it open and went through. Cal hesitated for a few seconds, then followed.

It was very peaceful inside, sheltered from the winter air, the stonework covered in the last of the summer clematis vines. It would be a paradise in the right season, he thought, all pink and white blossoms.

At the end of the garden there was a simple white marble stone with a gold inscription. In front of it was a vase of porcelain flowers that never wilted.

Marguerite dabbed her eyes with a

lace handkerchief.

'I'm glad you came, even if it took you a while.' She looked up at him. 'It wasn't your fault. It was an accident.'

'I try to tell myself that. But if I hadn't told her I was leaving her, none of this would've happened.' Cal felt the old anguish and guilt rise up.

'No, no, you can't blame yourself. My daughter was an accident waiting to happen. I loved her, but I wasn't blind to her faults. I told her that her obsession with you would come to no good. But she wouldn't listen. That day . . . when the police came to tell me about the accident . . . it's strange, but I almost guessed what they were going to say.

'You're making yourself unhappy for no reason, Cal. You've got to let it go. Move on.'

Cal stood there, and it was as if the air around him shifted. Marguerite's words got through to him. If she could admit Anthea's problems and forgive them as her mother, then couldn't he?

A great weight lifted from him. He felt his shoulder muscles almost physically ache as he stood straight.

'Don't let the accident define you. You have to learn to love and trust again. Your mother tells me you don't date any more. That's a waste for some girl.' There was warmth in Marguerite's voice as she gently teased him. 'How is your mother? I haven't seen her for some while.'

Cal's mother and Marguerite were old friends from the same social circle. It was how he'd met Anthea, at a party given right here in her family home.

'She's away in Bermuda with her new husband,' Cal said, trying not to let any bitterness ring through. It was typical of his mother. She couldn't stand illness or drama or any kind of event that might mean she had to do something she didn't like. Although she and Donal remained on good terms, she hadn't been to visit him once since his stroke. Instead, she'd whisked her third husband quickly away to their holiday home.

He couldn't imagine Lara behaving like that. Her first words on the phone had been concern for his father's wellbeing. Her sympathy had shone through even over the telephone line. She was kind and loving and empathic. Not to mention stunningly attractive and desirable.

He was driving away from the house when he suddenly braked and slewed the car into the side of the road. He stopped the engine, let the motor wind down, and kept his hands frozen to the wheel. He was an idiot. He'd denied his feelings too long. He didn't just *like* Lara. There was a reason his body ached with loneliness. He was in love with her.

Marguerite had given him closure over Anthea's death. Now he owed it to himself, and to Lara, to move on and to let her into his heart. The question was, could she love him too? He didn't know, but he knew he wanted a chance to find out.

His cell phone rang. It was Garrett.

'Cal, can you meet me back over at the hospital? The duty nurse just phoned. Dad spoke.'

'That's great news. I'm about a half-hour out of town. I'll get there as soon as I can.'

Cal turned the ignition and got the car moving fast along the highway. He didn't want to hope too much and be disappointed, but if Donal was speaking, surely that was a sign of great improvement.

He met Garrett in the small antechamber to Donal's private room. It was quiet on the floor. The nurses had been on their rounds distributing lunches to the patients, and there were usually no visitors allowed until the afternoon. But Donal was a special case. He'd made a miraculous leap forward in his recovery, and the nurses were delighted to share that with his sons.

Cal made to go through to see his father when Garrett held him back by the arm. 'Can I ask you something?'

Cal raised his eyebrows. 'Sure. But right now? Can't it wait until we've seen Dad?'

'I kinda want to get it sorted before we see him. In case he's in a position to make demands.'

'I think that's unlikely, but okay, let's hear it.' Cal sat on one of the leatherette benches and Garrett took the other opposite. His little brother looked serious for once.

'I want more authority at work. I want control of some of the business.'

Cal frowned. 'You've got some authority already. I'm not sure what you're asking for.'

'I've got limited authority under you. I can make some decisions, but ultimately I have to ask you for permission for certain actions.' Garrett stood up and paced the small space. He looked almost angry with Cal.

'The reason for that, as you know, is that while Dad is incapacitated, I'm head of the Enterprises,' Cal said patiently. 'I'm trying to protect you from the burden of being in charge.'

'But maybe I want that burden,' Garrett burst out, spinning on his heel to confront his brother.

Cal leaned back, consciously relaxing his posture. It wouldn't do any good to get into a slanging match at Donal's bedside. Besides, this was interesting coming from Garrett, who had never shown the slightest interest in the family business before.

'You do realise it means an awful lot of work? We're talking evenings and weekends. Would cut big-time into your partying.'

Garrett pulled a face. 'Cal, haven't you noticed? In the two months since you came home, I've not been to any wild parties. Those days are gone, brother. I've met a girl I really like.'

Now, Cal sat up straight. 'So this is what your request is about. Garrett, I think maybe you're finally growing up. Why haven't I met this girl?'

'It's pretty serious. I wanted to be

sure before I brought her home to meet the family. Then, with Dad's stroke and all, it wasn't the right time. But I need to work. No more playing about and wasting my trust fund.'

Cal nodded. 'Okay, you got it. From Monday, you take charge of some areas of work. We can sort out the details in the morning at the office.'

He was getting up to go in to see Donal when Garrett spoke again.

'There's someone special in your life too, isn't there? This Lara, over in Scotland. The way you spoke about her, I got the distinct impression you two were an item. So what happened?'

'Nothing happened. She was an employee at Invermalloch. We were . . . friends.'

Garrett made a disparaging noise and outstared his older sibling. 'Give me the truth. I'm your brother, I know you. She was more than a friend.'

Now it was Cal's turn to pace the room.

'You're right. Lara is special and I'm

in love with her. But I messed up. I told her there could be nothing between us. I was still hurting over Anthea, and I thought I couldn't fall in love and put myself through that again. I was a fool, and now I've lost her.'

'Lost her? What do you mean? Isn't she over there?'

'No, she's gone. Invermalloch's shut for the winter, and Lara's job was seasonal.'

'She must've left a forwarding address. She can't have vanished.'

But she has vanished.

'I've got a phone number.' A number Lara had given to Helen but not to him.

'So use it. What's the matter with you, Cal? It's not like you to give up so easily. Go after this girl. Tell her how you feel.'

'It's not that easy,' Cal said, shaking his head. 'I can't just up and leave here. Not while Dad's so ill. Then there's the Enterprises. They don't run themselves. I've got duties here that I can't run from.'

Garrett stood in front of him and placed his hands firmly on Cal's shoulders, forcing him to look him in the eye. Cal had forgotten they were on an equal height. His younger brother was all grown up, and there was no real physical difference now between them.

'We'll go and see Dad now. Yeah, he's not well, but it sounds like he's making a recovery. The medics said that once that recovery began, it could speed up. I can look after him. Besides, I'll have help. That girl I was telling you about, Mary, is a nurse. As to MacDonald Enterprises, don't you think it's time you let me take on that burden? It'll be great experience for me to be in full charge while you go find Lara. Trust me, Cal.'

And Cal did trust Garrett. He'd changed. Perhaps finding love with Mary had done it. Or he'd finally tired of parties and wasting his money and frittering his life away. Whatever it was, Cal saw a shaft of light at the end of the tunnel. He could leave New York. For a while, at least.

They went in then to see Donal. He was sitting up in bed, and there were fewer tubes and bleeping monitors than earlier. He managed a rasping greeting. It was hard to make out what he was saying, but that didn't matter. It was a small but vital step on his road to good health.

Cal excused himself after half an hour, leaving Garrett making a mostly one-sided conversation with some single utterings from Donal. He went out into the hospital car park and turned up his collar against the bitter cold. The grainy sky promised more snow. He wondered if it was snowing in the Highlands of Scotland.

Hesitantly he pulled out his cell phone and dialled the number Helen had given him. It rang and rang for the longest while, but Lara didn't answer it.

13

Lara pulled the front door of the cottage shut for the last time and locked it. There was a finality to her action which made her sad. She'd loved living there, and had made it her own over the summer and early autumn, so it felt like home. She'd miss the view out beyond the birch grove to the path, and further to the mountains. She remembered her hillwalking and her rescue by Cal.

Cal. There it was. The real reason for this deep sadness that choked her throat and sat like a bitter pill in her stomach. Their last conversation played on a loop in her head every time she thought of him. Which was all the time. She'd been worried for him. His father sounded so ill, and Cal had dropped everything to fly home to be at his bedside. She understood that. It was no less than what she expected from the man she had fallen in love with. Cal was honest and kind and caring. Of course he had to go back to New York. All his dreams of living and working at Invermalloch had to be put on hold.

But he'd sounded so formal over the telephone line. He'd thanked her for her hard work as countryside ranger. Spoken about the visitor attraction for next year. What about the kisses they'd shared? What about the night of passion high up under the mountain's shadow in the midst of a storm? She'd wanted to cry all this out to him, but instead she'd ended up sounding polite and officious, much like him. *Where will you go now?* he'd asked. But Lara didn't believe he really wanted to know. Instead, there was an implication in his voice that she *should* move on. There was nothing to keep her at Invermalloch now.

So she'd kept her answer vague. Which wasn't hard to do. The truth was, she had absolutely no idea what she was going to do next. This brief phase of her life was over. She had no plans for the future. It should've frightened her but she felt numb.

Lara put the cottage keys in her pocket and lifted up the two heavy bags. The last of her stuff. Malorie was waiting for her in the car, at the entrance to the estate, with the rest of Lara's belongings. She had wanted to be with Lara for the last sweep through the cottage to check if she'd left anything, but her sister had told her she wanted to do that alone.

Malorie had shaken her head. 'If that's your choice, fine. I'll take this suitcase and bung it in the boot. I can read my book in the car while I'm waiting, I suppose. Don't be long, will you?'

When Lara didn't answer, Malorie gave an exasperated sigh. 'What is the matter with you, Lara? You've had a face like a wet weekend since I came up to visit you. I thought you liked this place? Honestly, I wish I'd never bothered coming up. I've had a week of entertaining myself while you took your guided walks or whatever. I've never drunk so much coffee or read so many trashy magazines in my life. There's nothing to do up here. It's awful.'

'There's nothing the matter. I'm fine. And I'm sorry you've had such a terrible holiday up here. But I didn't ask you to come.'

Malorie tutted. 'You didn't ask me to come, I agree, but you needed me. I could tell. Besides, Jason told me you weren't acting like yourself.'

'You shouldn't listen to him,' Lara said sharply. 'For goodness' sake, can't you let it go? It's over with Jason. Why do you insist on keeping in touch with him and trying to get us back together?'

Malorie put on her pained-and-suffering elder-sister expression. 'I only want what's best for you. Mum and Dad are worried about you too.'

'What's best for me doesn't include Jason Wilmot,' Lara said plainly.

'We only want you to be happy.'

'Then let me be happy by finding my own way.'

'If only you knew what that was,' Malorie replied tartly. 'No, Lara. What's going to happen is you are going to finish up here, and then come and live with me and Tom until you decide what you want.'

Lara gritted her teeth at her older sister's bossiness, but a part of her was secretly glad that Malorie was taking control. After all, Lara *was* drifting. Now that Cal had gone, she didn't know what her path was going to be. Her time at Invermalloch was up. She might as well go and stay with Malorie until she made some serious decisions about her life. That these decisions wouldn't involve Cal made pains shoot through her as if a knife had been plunged into her.

She was relieved when Malorie stalked off, taking the moral high ground with her. The car was parked as close to the cottage as the tarmacked surfaces allowed. She waited until the blue Escort was driving away to the distant entrance off the old road. Lara had hardly been back on that road since the day Helen had stopped and given her a lift to Invermalloch. There was no need. She had everything she wanted here. Food deliveries came by truck to the lodge, and she'd been able to order what she needed through Helen. She'd been to the village for minor items, but that was it. The outside world had seemed far away and unimportant. Except that now she was going back to it.

★   ★   ★

'Do you like the new wallpaper in the hall?' Helen asked as Lara went into the lodge. 'Or is it too bright? I can't tell, I've seen it so often, but what will visitors' first impressions be?'

The hallway was looking bright and clean and inviting with its lemon-coloured walls. 'It's nice,' Lara said truthfully. 'Are you going ahead with

248

the visitor attraction, then?'

Helen looked puzzled. 'Why wouldn't we?'

'I just thought, with Cal gone ... ' There was a lump in Lara's throat that wouldn't budge.

'You don't think he's coming back?'

'Do you?'

Helen reached out for her and gave her a warm hug.

'You're in love with him, aren't you? Don't bother to deny it, Lara. I've seen the way the two of you got on over the months you've been here. I've also seen the way that Cal looks at you when you don't notice he's watching. Don't you think he's got feelings for you too?'

'I don't know,' Lara cried, the tears welling up. She rubbed them away fiercely. 'He doesn't seem to care whether I'm leaving or not.'

'He's got a lot on his mind right now, with Donal so ill,' Helen said gently. 'But I'm certain he'll be back.'

Lara felt dreadful. How selfish she was, crying over Cal when his father could be dying. She pulled herself together with a real effort. There had been a quiet reprimand in Helen's voice. And she was right.

Helen went on, 'Cal wasn't well when he arrived here at Invermalloch in the spring. His leg wasn't healing as quickly as it ought; and he had other scars too, deep inside, from his terrible accident and Anthea's actions. But you helped him. He was in a dark place before you arrived. You lifted his spirits and mended him. I'd say he loves you too. He just doesn't know it yet.'

'But there's no chance now that he will. It's over and he's gone and now I'm leaving,' Lara replied bleakly.

'It's winter now, but we're planning our grand opening event in March. I expect we'll need our countryside ranger in place for that. If you want the job, it's yours.' Helen smiled. 'You don't need to tell me now, but think about it, and keep in touch. A lot can happen in four months.'

'Thank you, Helen. For everything.'

It was Lara's turn to hug Helen. She was a good friend, and Lara would miss her.

'Don't go without leaving me your mobile phone number,' Helen said. 'I'll pass it along to Cal when he phones next, if you want me to.'

Lara wrote it on a scrap of paper and gave it to Helen. Would Cal phone? Or would he decide to let it lie? A summer romance that had faded to a wintry nothing.

Beyond the lodge, there was the impatient tooting of a car horn. Malorie waved agitatedly from the driver's window.

'That's my taxi calling me,' Lara said wryly. 'I'd better go.'

Her last sight of Invermalloch was of Helen waving from the grand old entrance as Malorie drove the car, stacked high with bags and boxes, out between the stone pillars and onto the icy Highland road.

★　★　★

It was a long journey south with traffic delays due to the snowy weather and a bad accident on the motorway near Glasgow. They stopped at a cheap hotel in the Midlands, and Lara endured a restless night, listening to the roar of traffic on the nearby highway that never ceased. She wondered if Cal heard traffic in his home in New York. He'd never spoken about his life there. Funny, that; all his talk was of memories of Invermalloch, as if that was where his heart lay. She knew nothing of his actual day-to-day life in America. Did he live alone? Or did he share a house with his brother Garrett and father Donal? Was his home in the city, or did they live in the suburbs or countryside?

No, he didn't live in the countryside, she decided, lying back on the lumpy hotel pillow, wide awake despite the late hour. Beside her, on the twin bed in the cramped room, Malorie's breathing was deep and even. She was exhausted from the driving even though they'd shared it, taking one hour at a time. Cal talked so passionately about the wilderness of the Highlands, he seemed like a thirsty man in a desert. So, she deduced, he lived in the city surrounded by traffic and people noise and the crammed atmosphere of the metropolis.

Lara had never been to the States. Her travelling had extended as far as Spain on family holidays, and lately there had never been enough money for going abroad. She and Jason had been saving for their own house, it brought home to her how different she and Cal were. He was rich and powerful and lived an international lifestyle. And she was just an English girl living an ordinary life. Why did she think he'd ever care for her? She rolled over in despair and tried to sleep.

The next day, they arrived tired and hungry at Malorie's small terraced house in Exeter.

'I don't have space to store all your stuff, so you'll have to take some over to

Mum and Dad's,' Malorie said, showing her into the tiny spare bedroom.
When she'd gone, Lara sank back onto
the bed and stared at the ceiling. She
was empty inside.

As the days passed, she settled into
life as Malorie's guest and as Tom's
auntie. The presence of Tom, who was
three, made everything bearable. He
was happy and energetic and insisted
on Auntie Lara playing every game
under the sun with him. She was
searching for jobs too, but there weren't
many on offer. Too many times in a day,
she took out her mobile and checked it
for messages. But there were never any.
Cal had forgotten her. His life in New
York would be busy with Donal and his
work. Or had he met someone?

Lara tortured herself in this fashion
every day. Eventually she phoned
Helen, to keep in touch and find out
how the renovations were getting on.

'They're finished. Can you believe it?
The workmen and their vans and
ladders and hammering have all gone.

It's fantastic. I wish you could see it.'
Helen's voice was cheerful. It was lovely
to hear her. It brought back all Lara's
memories of the summer.

'What's the weather like up there?' In
Devon there was a mild sleet blowing
down the road. Lara watched it as she
listened to Helen's chat.

'There's a foot or more of snow over
the whole estate. The snow plough is
out daily, keeping us linked to the rest
of the world. It's magical, though. The
mountains are glistening with the new
fall today.'

Lara wanted to ask about Cal but
could barely bring herself to do so.
'Have there been any calls from the
States?'

'Yes, Cal rang yesterday. His father is
improving, but slowly. He asked
whether I'd heard from you, but I told
him I hadn't. I'll let him know you've
phoned.'

'Don't do that, Helen. Really. If he
wants to call, he's got my number.'

And clearly he didn't want to call,

because he never had. Lara's pride wouldn't let her phone him. She couldn't bear it if he rejected her over the line.

★ ★ ★

The winter became colder and harsher, even in the south. Lights were hoisted up by the council, strung along the city streets, and Christmas trees began to appear in windows and shopping centres. It all depressed Lara. She could not get into the holiday spirit at all. She moped instead, driving Malorie mad by shutting her bedroom door and keeping away from everyone.

'That's it, I've had enough,' Malorie announced, flinging the door open and startling Lara, who was reading the newspaper and searching for jobs — unsuccessfully. No-one was advertising posts so close to Christmas. 'Get down here and help me prepare the turkey for tomorrow. Or you can cut crosses into a hundred sprouts if you prefer. Anything but sit in this bloody bedroom one more day.'

It was while they were down in Malorie's cosy kitchen, making bread-crumbs for the herb stuffing, that Malorie dropped her bombshell.

'Finn's joining us tomorrow for Christmas Day.'

She didn't look at Lara when she said it, just kept her head down and sprinkled the dried herbs onto the bowl of crumbs.

'What! You asked your ex-husband to come and celebrate Christmas?'

'Don't look so shocked. If you noticed anything around you instead of sitting in the bedroom, then you'd know we were back in touch. And Finn's still my husband. We didn't get around to filing for divorce.'

Lara was ashamed. She hadn't being taking notice of Malorie at all. She hadn't asked where her sister was going on the evenings she'd gladly babysat for Tom.

'Are you two getting back together?'

Malorie shrugged, but a little smile hovered on her lips. The stuffing was now thoroughly mixed, so Lara pushed the bowl away and put her hands on her hips.

'Well?'

'Oh, all right.' Malorie blew out a breath. 'We've had a few cautious dates and we like what we see. I never stopped loving him, you know.'

'Does he love you?'

'Yes, he does. He admits he was being immature when we broke up over him needing his space. He's travelled for two years and got it out of his system. Now he's ready to be a husband and a father to Tom.'

Privately, Lara thought Finn was a jerk. But Malorie looked so happy that she didn't voice her thoughts. Besides, Tom needed his father. He was a lovely little boy, but boisterous and exhausting. Lara knew Malorie found it tough being a single parent.

'Good luck,' Lara said, and meant it.

Malorie looked uncomfortable.

'The thing is, Finn's going to be moving back into the house.'

'And you need me to move out,' Lara finished for her.

★ ★ ★

Where would she go? Her heart sank. Malorie's house had been a bolthole for her. She wasn't ready to move on. But she wasn't being fair. Lara gave her sister a bright smile. 'Not a problem. When do you want me out by?'

'Are you sure? You don't mind? I feel terrible throwing you out.'

'Don't be daft. Most of my stuff is at the parents' anyway. I can be cleared out very quickly.'

'Where will you go? It's not as if Mum and Dad can take you in. They're renting their spare room to a lodger for holiday savings.'

That was true. Their parents had always longed for a round-the-world cruise, and had finally decided next year was the time. They were saving like mad to go on their once-in-a-lifetime holiday. Lara had agreed that next year she'd keep an eye on their property.

'Look, don't worry about me. Something will turn up. I'm going to enjoy Christmas, and on Boxing Day I'll start to plan what I'm going to do. Okay?'

She kissed Malorie's cheek, and felt her relax at her casual answer. She didn't let her sister see how devastating the news was. But when she went upstairs to get out of her food-stained jersey, Lara began to have a change of heart.

She sat down heavily on the bed. It seemed like everyone was moving on, changing, while she stayed the same. Her parents were going on a six-month cruise, making the most of their retirement years while they were still relatively fit. Malorie was getting back together with the man she loved. Making a family for Tom.

And Lara? She'd given up so easily on what she wanted. She'd let fear of rejection stand in her way, and never phoned Cal to tell him how she really felt. He was nothing like Jason. She understood that, had done for quite some time. So was she going to fight for what she wanted most in life? She wasn't a quitter. She was a stubborn fighter. Okay, she had acted like a wuss recently, but that was about to change! She was going to call Cal and tell him that she loved him. See what he did with that. If he didn't feel anything for her, then she was going to deal with it.

Malorie shouted up the stairs.

'Come quickly. It's Helen calling from Invermalloch. She needs your help!'

14

Invermalloch Estate was like a winter wonderland. All the familiar shapes — the lodge, the stables and outbuildings, the workers' cottages — were softened into hummocks by the heavy layers of snow. The sun shone down, making the surfaces sparkle like cut glass.

Lara turned from the heavenly view from the bay window, and began to build up the fire in the formal dining room. She glanced at her watch. Once she'd made the fire up with coal and wood for the evening, she was due at the courtyard to meet the group for bird-watching. There were great northern divers and red-necked phalaropes on Loch Malloch, bird rarities that the guests would be pleased to be shown.

Helen rushed in to the room with pots of holly sprays and amaryllis.

'Remind me again why Mr Gainwath is here,' Lara said, rocking back on her heels to admire her construction of kindling. Her hands were black with coaldust and there was more than a speck of it on her trouser knees.

'Because he's impossibly, implausibly rich,' Helen said breathlessly. 'And when he asked if he could hire the lodge for a winter party, I knew that I had to say yes. The money he's paying will come in extremely useful next year.'

'It's an awful lot of work, keeping four people happily fed and entertained. I'm beginning to feel like a Victorian maid!'

'You don't regret coming to help me, do you?' Helen looked dismayed.

Lara laughed. 'No, of course not. I'm exaggerating. You did me a favour. I was on the brink of having nowhere to live. Your phone call came just at the right moment. It helped me get through Christmas Day, knowing I'd be heading north afterwards. I'm really happy for Malorie and Finn, but playing gooseberry isn't my style.'

There was a silence then. Lara was thinking of Cal. Where was he? What was he doing? She tried to imagine what Christmas in New York would be like. Helen must have read her thoughts, because she spoke first.

'I haven't heard from him this week. It's funny, he usually makes contact regularly for updates on the estate. It must be because of the holidays. And of course, Donal is making a very good recovery; they hope to get him home soon.'

'That's a relief,' Lara said.

It sounded as if Cal would be needed over there for quite some time to come. But what had she expected? She hadn't phoned him after all. Helen's call for help had distracted her; and what with Christmas, then travelling north in precarious weather conditions, and the all-consuming duties of looking after Mr Gainwath, his wife and their friends, she hadn't gone near her mobile phone until yesterday.

When she did try Cal's number, she got no reception. The bad weather in the Highlands had disrupted service. Maybe it was for the best, she told herself. Cal had clearly forgotten about her. But it hurt. Had their night together meant so little to him?

Helen interrupted her musings.

'Lara, sorry, but you need to get moving. They're going to be waiting for you in the next few minutes for the birdwatching. It's freezing out there, so don't forget your scarf, hat and gloves. The new telescope is in the hallway.'

* * *

Her feet crunched on fresh snow as she made her way to the courtyard. The telescope was balanced on her shoulder and her breath was like smoke in front of her. Lara had never experienced such bitter northern cold. But she liked it. It sharpened her mind and made her concentrate on the here and now, instead of what had been and what might have been.

'Ah, there she is. We're looking forward to seeing something special,' Mr Gainwath boomed cheerfully, rubbing his gloved hands together. 'What have you got lined up for us, young lady?'

'There are plenty of water birds on the loch.' Lara smiled. 'If you could all please follow me, we'll go down there now and see what there is. The path's been gritted, but watch your step for ice.'

That had been her first task of the day, out with a bucket of sand and a shovel to grit the path to Loch Malloch. She'd revelled in the hard physical labour that allowed no room for thought.

The loch was half-covered in a sheet of ice, but thankfully there was sufficient water exposed for the birds to float on. Lara set up the telescope so that the guests could get good close-up views of the waterfowl. The striking patterns on the divers' necks glowed in the magnifying disc, and people crowded round to look into it, or stood with individual binoculars to scan the loch surface.

Lara felt surplus to requirements. She'd done her bit: explaining about the birds, how to identify them, what they ate and where they nested in the summer. She'd stood back then, allowing the group to enjoy their discoveries of nature. Looking out on the winter loch, it seemed impossible that she and Cal had fished here under hot summer sunshine. The same day he'd announced he was staying in Scotland and running the estate. Dreams that had almost instantly had crumbled to dust with the news of his father's ill-health.

She half-saw a movement out of the corner of her eye. Turning, she saw a tall figure making its way down between the dark trees towards the loch. She stared and her heart thumped in her chest. It looked like . . . but that was impossible.

But it was. It was Cal.

Lara dropped her binoculars and began to run. She met him halfway, just where the forest gave way to the open land and the lochside.

'You came back. When . . . how . . . ?'

Cal looked at her with such intensity that Lara's insides melted. He didn't say anything, but pulled her to him and kissed her hard. She opened her mouth under the pressure of his, and kissed him back just as deeply. There was so much that needed saying, but it could wait. Her body needed this. She wrapped her arms around him, and he moulded her form to the hard, lean length of his. Finally, she drew back with a ragged breath.

'Why are you here?'

Cal stroked her hair back from her face and let his lips touch her brow, her nose, linger on her mouth before answering.

'I came to find you. You didn't answer my call and I had no address. So

I came back here in the hope of tracing you.'

'You called me? I didn't get it.' But then she remembered that her battery had gone dead and she'd had to replace it. She must have lost messages and calls in that period. Anyway, it didn't matter because Cal was here, really here. Her whole body felt alive, truly alive for the first time in months.

'You never got in contact with me.' He sounded hurt, and Lara realised that he'd been hiding the depth of that pain.

'I couldn't. It was too complicated.' She shook her head. How could she explain what she had felt? That she was in love with him, but knew he didn't care for her that way?

There was a shout from the loch. Cal stared over to it.

'Looks like your services are required. You'd better go and help. We'll talk later.'

'Did Helen explain about Mr Gain-wath and his party?'

'Yes, she did, and I approve whole-heartedly. We used to hire out the lodge for parties years ago, but not recently.' He let go of her hands.

Lara was reluctant to leave him. She'd a fleeting fear that he'd disappear if he went out of her sight. There was so much to discuss. Mr Gainwath shouted up to her again and she had to go.

'Wait, Cal,' she cried. 'Where will I see you?'

'Up at the house after your bird-watching. Helen tells me there's to be a dinner then. After that, we can talk.'

Lara had to be patient, answering the party's questions about birds and wildlife. But, inside, she was champing at the bit to get back to the lodge to see Cal.

★　★　★

There was a roaring, crackling fire in the hearth that gave out a tremendous heat. Mr Gainwath's face was positively ruddy in the firelight, from both the flames' warmth and too much excellent wine. The noise of the guests' chatter rushed about the large room.

Mrs McGaddie did her best, serving up dishes of hot venison stew, and Lara and Helen discreetly helped her. Lara was aware of Cal's presence wherever she was. He sat at the head of the table, making polite conversation with his wealthy guests.

Lara wanted dinner to be finished and gone. She needed to find out what Cal felt about her. Had he changed? He looked impossibly handsome tonight, with his dark hair, and those intense blue eyes that sought her out whenever he could. He wore a formal shirt and tie for the dinner, and a charcoal suit which made him look dangerously attractive.

Lara knew she looked good. She'd lost weight that winter, and her green velvet dress fitted her perfectly, outlining her slim waist. She'd matched it with high-heeled sandals, pleased with the extra height they gave her.

Cal's fingers brushed lightly against hers as she helped Helen remove the dinner plates. Her skin tingled and she longed to run her fingers over his, to stroke and touch his muscled forearms and feel the thick tension of his hair. She didn't care whether he loved her or not. Her love for him was stronger than ever. But would a passionate affair be enough?

After dinner, she excused herself. In traditional manner, the men had retired to the living room where an equally large hot fire was burning. The two ladies in the party lingered over drinks in the dining room, chatting with Helen and asking interested questions about the estate and the harshness of the climate.

Lara went upstairs to her room. It was the same she'd first used at the lodge the day she'd arrived looking for work. It all seemed so long ago. It was neatly laid out, and she'd packed away her belongings. Helen had told her she was welcome to stay as long as she wanted to. In fact, she'd added that she was hoping Lara would stay on until the March opening event. There was work to do over the winter to pay her way. Lara was happy to work for a place to stay and her meals, until she could ranger again in spring.

She sat on her bed, unsure what to do. She wanted Cal near her. Wanted to hear what he had to say. There was a creak of floorboards outside her door, and then he was there.

'I've escaped.' He grinned at her. 'They're so merry on my best wine that I won't be missed.'

Suddenly, the room felt too small. She could smell his aftershave, something rich and spicy and quintessentially Cal. His jacket rustled as he threw it off over the chair back. He sat next to her on the bed.

'I'm sorry we couldn't talk before. Events kept conspiring to keep us apart,' he said.

She waited. He took her hand, played with her fingers. A fire leapt between them but he didn't move away. She felt every whorl of his fingertips and the burning trail of her nerve-endings, from the tips to the very centre of her body. It was a delightful, dangerous torture, especially as she had no idea what he felt about her.

'Why did you come back to look for me?' she whispered, almost dreading the answer.

'We said we'd be friends, didn't we,' Cal said slowly, his blue gaze penetrating. 'But I don't want to be friends any more.'

'You don't?' Hope flickered uncertainly as his lips grazed hers; she couldn't look away from him.

His mouth hovered over hers, but then he leaned back and she felt the loss of him. He didn't know the power he had over her. The ache in her body that wouldn't cease when he was near. But she had to hear what he had to say.

'When I went back to the States, I was in turmoil,' Cal said, taking her hands in his and looking at her straight on, willing her to understand. 'My father was so ill, and I was scared I'd lose him. But a part of me was angry with him too. I'd just made my decision to stay at Invermalloch and run the estate as a going concern. The renovations were underway. And you were there. I was angry that I had to leave all that and go home.

'It didn't hit me until I was back in New York how much I'd come to depend on you. You were always about at Invermalloch, quietly working with your groups. I could see you whenever I wanted. Then suddenly there was an ocean between us. I missed you so much, it was like a punch to the gut.'

'But you didn't call to tell me that. I thought that you didn't care.' She curled her fingers into his and his grip tightened. It was as if now he'd found her, he was never going to let her go.

'I couldn't call. I had to work things out for myself.' Cal sighed and twisted his mouth in self-blame. 'When I saw my father so weak, fighting for his life and for good health, it struck me how short and sweet life is. We don't get a lot of it. I needed to get closure on my relationship with Anthea, so I went to see her mother. I'd kept away from her since the funeral because I couldn't bear to see the accusation in her eyes. That I killed her daughter.'

'But she forgave you,' Lara said, knowing it had to be true. Cal hadn't killed Anthea. It was clear that she'd brought her misfortune down on herself. Even as her mother grieved, she would have to know that.

Cal nodded. 'She forgave me. And it was as I was leaving that I realised that I was thinking of you every moment of every day, and that it wasn't because I'd left a friend behind.'

He moved closer to Lara, cupping her face gently with his large hands, and locking gazes with her.

'Why was it?' she asked, daring him to answer. Scarcely hoping for the reply she wanted, *needed*, to hear.

'It was because I'd fallen deeply in

love with you, my darling.' Cal leaned towards her and kissed her tenderly, with such deep emotion that she felt the tears well in her eyes.

'I love you too,' she cried, returning his kisses with increasing passion. She broke away to try to explain. 'I thought, after Jason, that I could never love another man. But it didn't take me long to figure out you were nothing like him.'

'When did you know you loved me?' he demanded, slipping the clasps from her hair so that it flowed like pale honey over her shoulders.

'That night under the hills,' Lara replied, sliding a glance at him, her face warming at the memories of their passion. 'I knew it then.'

'Mmm, that night was magical.' Cal's lips burned a pattern of light kisses along the curve of her neck. 'It's a pity you don't need warming tonight.'

'Oh, I don't know . . . ' Lara leaned back on the bed. 'It's pretty cold in here, given there's no fire and only a rattly old radiator.'

'I can't have you succumbing to hypothermia under my roof,' Cal said sternly. His fingers found the fastening of her dress and he slid the material down.

There were goosebumps on Lara's shoulders, and she shivered — but not from cold. She unbuttoned Cal's shirt and slid her hand over his muscled chest. He groaned, and pulled her on top of him.

* * *

Afterwards, Cal pulled the duvet over them and they lay snugly together in the bed, warmed by their body heat and the passion wrapped around them. Lara's head lay in the crook of his arm, so comfortably as if they'd been made perfectly in size for each other.

She could barely believe her happiness. She was so deeply in love with Cal. And he returned that love. The spectres of Anthea and Jason had fled into the ether; and the laird and the ranger were ready to commit to each other forever.

She gave a contented breath out and snuggled in to him. Cal put his arm more firmly round her.

'You're going to love New York,' he murmured sleepily. 'I can't wait to show you my home there, and introduce you to my father and to Garrett. If you don't like the house, then we'll move out of the city. I don't care. As long as I've got you.'

Lara's eyes opened wide. She turned out of his embrace, and stared at him.

'New York? I can't go and live in America. What about my family? I can't just leave them. What about Invermalloch? I thought you were coming back to live here.'

They stared at each other in mutual disbelief.

15

Lara was miserable. How had it gone so terribly wrong? She was standing in the big, airy kitchen, chopping vegetables for the midday meal. It was the kind of task that required absolutely no mental effort, simply repetitive movement and an end result. Which was all that Lara could manage right now. Her head ached from thinking about Cal and the horrible argument they'd had last night.

Beside her, preparing marinades for the meal, Helen shot her a sympathetic glance. Although neither Lara nor Cal had mentioned any falling-out, it was obvious from their stiff manner with each other that they had argued.

'Do you want to talk about it?' Helen asked softly, pushing the mixing bowl away from her and turning to Lara with worried eyes.

Lara shook her head and felt ready

tears touch her cheek. She rubbed them away.

'I don't understand,' Helen went on helplessly. 'He came back for you, Lara. I couldn't believe it when I saw him arrive at the lodge. He loves you. And you love him. So what can possibly be wrong?'

'It's not that simple,' Lara cried. 'Oh, Helen, I love Cal with all my heart, but what he's asking me to do is impossible. He wants me to give up my life here and move with him to America.'

They'd had such a heated argument, leaving them both bewildered. One moment they were together in Lara's bed, warm and drowsy and secure in the knowledge of a future together, and the next they were both sitting bolt upright with a gulf widening between them as a vast as the Atlantic.

'If you truly loved me, you wouldn't ask me to leave here,' Lara had said through numb lips.

'If you loved me, you'd follow me anywhere on the globe to be with me,' was Cal's bitter retort.

He couldn't seem to realise the enormity of what he was asking. Maybe it was because he had travelled so easily all his life between Britain and America. He had two homes, after all: one at Invermalloch and one in New York. But Lara didn't have that experience. In fact, she reminded herself sharply, she had no home at all. When she'd said that to Cal, he told her that that was all the more reason why she could come to New York and live.

'Why do I have to follow you?' Lara had parried, feeling stung by his logic. 'We're not living in the Dark Ages when a woman always follows her man. If you love me, then why don't you follow me to England, or stay with me here in the Highlands?'

At that, Cal had pushed himself angrily from her bed and not spoken until he'd put his clothes on. She'd had to face his rigid back instead. Then he'd turned, and looked not angry, but unutterably sad. That was worse. It twisted up Lara's insides and made her want to beg him to lie back down with her so they could cuddle and twine their bodies together in comfort and love. So that they could unsay the bitter words they had shouted to each other.

'I'm not some kind of throwback, Lara. I don't believe that a wife should follow her husband without thought. But you know how ill my father is. I can't move country, lock, stock and barrel, when he needs me. I hoped . . . I dreamed that you and I could set up home together; that you'd get to know my father and Garrett, and learn to love them the way I do. But I was wrong. I'm sorry.'

He got up slowly, not looking at her, and went out, closing the door quietly and firmly behind him. Lara stared at the paintwork and then lay back on the bed and sobbed. She cried so much that her eyes hurt and she felt sick. It wasn't just what had been said. It was the pain and sadness in Cal's gaze as he spoke. She wanted to take it all back, but she also wanted him to understand her feelings. Couldn't he see what he was asking of her?

He had been stiff and polite with her that morning when they unavoidably met in the hallway. Lara felt terrible. She hadn't slept for her torrent of thoughts and emotions, and was very glad when Helen called her into the kitchen to help. But now, Helen's kindness was undoing her. In a moment, if she didn't watch out, she'd cry all over the vegetables and spoil everyone's lunch.

'I'm sorry, I've got to go for walk and get some fresh air,' she said, untying her apron and putting it on the worktop.

She was nearly out of the door when Helen called to her. She looked back at the woman who had become her friend, and who was a loyal comrade and employee to Cal.

'Take my advice and don't act rashly. You may have to live with your regrets for a very long time.'

Lara crunched through the deep, crisp snow with Helen's warning ringing in her ears. She shoved her frozen fingers deep into her pockets, and tucked her chin into the warm fur collar of her coat. The surface of Loch Malloch was almost entirely covered by a sheet of ice today, which had encroached further in the intensely cold night. A few unhappy ducks stood on the solid surface, huddled together with ruffled feathers.

I don't believe a wife should follow her husband without thought, Cal had said in response to her words.

He wanted to marry her. She curled her fingers into her palms to warm them and began to walk restlessly along the edge of the icy water. She could be Mrs Lara MacDonald. She could *belong* to Cal. If only she had the courage to do so. There, she'd admitted it. She was scared of what he was asking her to do. To take a step into the unknown with him. She loved him so much. But she would miss her parents and Malorie and Tom if she went. She'd lose the familiarity of her own culture.

Her steps cracked the ice on the loch edge, leaving sounds like shots echoing in the air. She was kidding herself. These were reasons not to go, yes, but she was courageous enough to overcome them. Hadn't she left England for the unknown quantity that was the Scottish Highlands, on nothing more than the stab of a pin into a map?

Lara sighed and stared out over the wintry landscape. Wasn't her real fear that she might not live up to Cal's expectations? His lifestyle and life experiences were so very different from hers. He was well-travelled, a high-flyer in business, and used to the best society that New York could offer. Lara was none of those things. What if she wasn't cut out for his life in the States? He'd made it quite clear that was where they would live. If she didn't, then where did that leave her and their relationship?

She trudged back up to the lodge,

not any clearer in her mind as to what to do. All she knew was that she loved Cal deeply and without end. She didn't want a lifetime of regretting what might have been.

She stopped abruptly. Cal was standing there in the hall, looking at her. With a jolt of fear, she saw there were two suitcases at his feet.

'You're leaving?' she gasped.

'I'm going back,' he said, 'But . . . '

She cut in over him. 'But you only just got here. I know we argued, Cal, but you're seriously going? Without any fight in you?'

Why was he smiling? How dare he have such warmth in his blue eyes? He moved in close to her and, without asking, took a long kiss which stole her breath.

There was a pause after the kiss while Lara breathed again. She frowned and opened her mouth to speak, but Cal beat her to it. He held up his hand to stop her.

'You stood up to me just now the way

you did the very first day we met. Do you remember? You wanted to stroke Kinash and I asked you to stop.'

Where is he going with this? She didn't want to be reminded of how they'd met, and the searing attraction she'd immediately felt for him. If it was all to end right now, then let it happen without prolonging her agony.

But Cal was still speaking. And she had to listen.

'The only thing that matters is that I am in love with you, and always will be. Last night . . . I should've thought it all through before I discussed with you where we would live. I assumed too much. I knew you didn't have a place to stay, and I imagined . . . I hoped you'd like my place in New York. But I had a lot of thinking space last night after I left you. Heck, I didn't sleep one wink for thinking on what you said. And you were right. I can't expect you to leave your life here entirely.'

Lara broke in impatiently, desperate to explain herself. 'I had all night to come to a decision too. I was scared, Cal. That I might not fit into your life in America. I'm not like Anthea, or other women you've dated previously. I don't think I'd be very good at glittering parties or hosting business dinners.'

Cal laughed. It was a free and happy sound. He shook his head at her puzzled look and swept her up into his arms.

'I thank God you're nothing like Anthea or my previous girlfriends, my darling. I don't care a jot about parties or business dinners. And I don't care one whit where we live as long as we're together.'

'But . . . the suitcases?' Lara stammered, squirming in delight inside his strong grasp, but still confused. 'Aren't you going back to the States? You said you couldn't leave your father, and it was wrong of me to ask you to. I'm . . . I'm coming with you, Cal. If you'll have me.'

His answer was a long, deep and hot kiss that had her clamouring for more.

He lifted his lips from hers reluctantly.

'I'm going back to the States. But I'm going back to make sure my father has all the excellent care he needs, and that Garrett is coping with his new responsibilities. Once I've settled my affairs, I'm going to ask you where in the whole world my darling wife would like to live.'

'Wife?' Lara said, pulling him closer and insisting on another molten kiss. 'Did you just ask me . . . ?'

At that point, Cal cut their embrace rudely short, leaving Lara dizzy and light-headed. He went down on one bended knee, and she was about to remark on how good it was to see his leg healed, when he asked her a question she had no hesitations, no qualms and no regrets in answering.

Epilogue

It was summer at Invermalloch. One of those rare scorching periods when the Highlands are at their best and every white sand beach, turquoise bay and wild moor looks like paradise. To first-time visitors to Scotland, it was astonishing that it wasn't teeming with crowds.

'I can't believe we've never visited this beautiful country before,' an American tourist told Cal as her husband took image after image on his tablet. 'We're sure coming back next year. Your lodge will be open, won't it?'

Cal assured her that the lodge would indeed be open. He hid a smile as he heard the tourist exclaim to the rest of her party about the blessed lack of mosquitos.

'She might get a horrible shock if next summer has normal weather. The midges do love the mild, rainy days, don't they,' Lara's voice whispered behind him.

Cal turned to his wife. She looked stunning as usual. Her pale blonde hair was loose to her shoulders, and she suited the blue cotton dress and flimsy sandals. He bent to kiss her and put a protective hand to the swell under her maternity wear.

'How's Fiona?' he asked teasingly.

'You're so sure it's going to be a girl?' Lara tossed back her hair and wrinkled her nose at him. 'Whereas I think that young Donal is fine, thank you very much.'

Cal's heart pressed close to his chest with his love for Lara. It didn't matter to him whether they had a girl or a boy for their firstborn. The only thing that mattered was how much he loved his wife.

'Talking of Donal, when's your father going to arrive?' Lara said, sounding slightly nervous.

Cal and Lara had missed the initial

grand opening of Invermalloch Lodge to public viewing last spring for two reasons. The first was that Donal had had a small setback to his recovery, and both of them felt they couldn't leave him. Once he began to make slow progress again, Cal and Lara arranged a small family wedding in New York in the spring. It had coincided with Invermalloch's March opening event, but they had kept up to date with what happened by an internet connection to Helen Thorpe and Bob Stanton, who told them it had been a roaring success.

Now it was over a year later, and finally they were back in their beloved Highlands. Not only that, but Donal and Garrett and his fiancée were coming to visit them.

The only problem was that Cal's father was still pressing them to settle in the States, and had even gone so far as to send them brochures of houses for sale near his own. Lara hoped very much that this visit would show Donal what a gorgeous place Invermalloch was, and how perfect it was to bring up their little family when it arrived.

Cal had kept his promise, and when he'd organised his businesses just the way he wanted them and made sure that Garrett was coping, he asked Lara where in the world she would like to live.

There was only one answer to that, and she'd seen the answering gleam in his eye when she told him. So they had come home to Invermalloch to face yet another biting winter and late spring. But it was all worth it, because the reward for the cold, dark months was this fantastic, unbeatable summer.

A sleek black car drew up to the lodge, scattering the wandering tourists. 'My father's here,' Cal said, and took Lara's hand tightly so they could go down the steps to greet him.

The old man got out of the car slowly, refusing any help from Garrett, who had rushed round from the driver's seat to get him. Mary was quick to follow. Donal stretched himself slowly upright after the long journey in the car and looked at his older son.

'Let's get you inside to a seat,' Garrett said, trying to take his father's arm.

'I'm fine, I'm fine.' The old man waved him off impatiently.

Garrett exchanged a look with Cal. Lara's heart sank. Donal wasn't smiling. In fact, he looked downright grim. Beside her, she felt Cal tense up.

Taking a deep breath, she left her husband, and — as lightly as possible, given her lately-increased girth — went down the steps with her hands out in welcome.

'Hello Donal, you're looking well. Won't you come inside for a refreshment? We can avoid the tearoom and take our drinks in the private rooms beyond.' She was talking too fast, she knew. But he seemed to relax, and took her hand and gripped it. Garrett gave her an encouraging wink and Mary looked relieved.

'Well, look at this old place. I haven't

stepped foot inside it in I don't know how long. Never got around to it somehow, once I was grown. Always thought it a godforsaken sort of place with no kinda civilization,' Donal rasped.

A silence bloomed between them all. Lara saw Cal's disappointed face. Garrett practically leapt up the stone steps to greet his brother and attempt to change the family's mood. Mary smiled sympathetically at Lara. Garrett and Mary knew just how much it meant to Cal and Lara that Donal accepted what they wanted for their future. But the old man could be, as Cal put it, ornery.

'Why don't I go and get the drinks, and we can have them out here?' Mary said nicely, indicating the newly-finished landscaped lawn in front of the lodge that Lara was so proud of.

She had designed it so that she and Cal could sit on the carved oak benches with a view to her little white cottage and its grove of birches, and let their vision follow the path to the pools and the foothills before it got lost in the wilderness of mountains beyond. It was a very special place to sit, and the lawns were cordoned off, preventing public access.

'Thanks Mary,' she said gratefully.

Donal let himself be guided to one of the oak benches by Cal. Garrett went inside to help his fiancée.

Lara and Cal sat with the old man and waited. Cal took her hand and she felt his warm strength connect with her. Whatever happened to them in the future, she always had her husband. She squeezed his fingers, and felt his tighten over hers instinctively.

There was a pause, and then Donal said, 'You've done good, son. You and Lara. Can I come visit you often?'

We do hope that you have enjoyed reading this large print book.

Did you know that all of our titles are available for purchase?

We publish a wide range of high quality large print books including:
Romances, Mysteries, Classics
General Fiction
Non Fiction and Westerns

Special interest titles available in large print are:
The Little Oxford Dictionary
Music Book, Song Book
Hymn Book, Service Book

Also available from us courtesy of Oxford University Press:
Young Readers' Dictionary
(large print edition)
Young Readers' Thesaurus
(large print edition)

For further information or a free brochure, please contact us at:
Ulverscroft Large Print Books Ltd.,
The Green, Bradgate Road, Anstey,
Leicester, LE7 7FU, England.
Tel: (00 44) **0116 236 4325**
Fax: (00 44) **0116 234 0205**